MW01118180

WITHDRAWN

A
PAPER MASK

Also by John Collee

Kingsley's Touch

A
PAPER MASK
JOHN COLLEE

ARBOR HOUSE
WILLIAM MORROW
New York

Library of Congress Cataloging-in-Publication Data

Collee, John.
    A paper mask / John Collee.
      p. cm.
    ISBN 1-55710-026-8
    I. Title.
    PR6053.0423P37 1989
    823′.914—dc19   88-21797
                                                           CIP

Printed in the United States of America

First U.S. Edition

1 2 3 4 5 6 7 8 9 10

BOOK DESIGN BY NICOLA MAZZELLA

A
PAPER MASK

CHAPTER
1

IF YOU WERE TO ASK ME what's the one thing I most clearly remember of those seven months it's the sensation of terror—my hands pouring sweat and my heart smashing about behind my ribs like the clapper of a bell. Toward the end I learned to dissociate myself from it—it was somebody else's nightmare, Hennessey's nightmare, I would be somewhere else entirely. But of the start I can remember every detail—the parquet floor, the whorled pattern on the rug and the black marble clock on the mantelpiece. It felt uncomfortably warm in the waiting room. I'd tried to open the windows only to find that they'd been nailed shut. Outside an inch of snow covered the lawn, the trees and the stone balustrades. Inside my cotton vest felt like wool and my woolen suit like sackcloth. I'd already flicked through all the magazines. I found it impossible to read, impossible even to concentrate on the pictures. I'd tried to rehearse the interview in my head but couldn't imagine what they'd ask. My concentration had gone and logical thought with it.

Beyond the snow-covered pines, Clifton was a glittering castle of snow and sandstone. I could leave now and they'd probably not miss me. I picked up my coat and started toward the door but was pulled up short by the thought of returning to West Harwood and the months of misery I'd already endured there. Stay? Go? I've never been able to make a decision. My life has always been controlled by accidents.

Go. Go! The whole thing was madness. I should never have come.

But what if someone saw me leaving? If the bloody windows opened I could have climbed out and fled across the lawn. I tried them once more but they wouldn't move. I picked up my coat and crossed to the door again, it opened before I reached it.

"Dr. Hennessey?"

I've never believed in love at first sight or at any other time for that matter, but once in a while you meet a total stranger who makes the bottom of your stomach fall away.

"They'll see you now," she said.

She had dark red hair, a pale face, and a gaze of such untrammeled clarity that it took your breath away. This may sound extravagant but remember, it was the first impression of a man in a state of mindless panic. Anxiety and sexual attraction are closely related—the breathlessness, the tremor, the sweating and confusion—maybe they're the same thing.

Anyway, what could I do but go with her? She walked beside me—close enough for me to smell her perfume. At times she would steer me in the correct direction by lightly touching my arm.

"What's your name?" I asked.

"Christine."

"I'm Simon. Have they appointed anyone yet?"

"Not yet. You're still in with a chance."

"Good." My own voice was thin and hoarse. I failed to inject it with any enthusiasm.

"This way," she said.

We emerged into a colonnaded courtyard. I could see steam rising from the hospital kitchens and billowing into the crystal sky. Above the colonnade there were two stories of arched windows. Snow had gathered on their lintels and in a thin blade along the wire mesh that surrounded the tennis court. There was ivy growing up this fence and a thin border of evergreen shrubs around it. Near to the hospital building the snow had melted back and was dripping from the eaves above our heads.

"Left here."

She led me back into the hospital through a half-glazed door. The sign above it said "ADMINISTRATIVE OFFICES." I tried to get rid of the gum I was chewing and found it harder to swallow than I'd anticipated. We had stopped outside an elaborately carved doorway.

"This is it. Good luck."

She knocked and turned the handle. I wanted to thank her but she had already turned away from me. The double doors swung apart. I hesitated on the threshold, unwilling, even then, to make the first truly irrevocable step. But in reality I had crossed that line two weeks previously. . . .

CHAPTER
2

"Do you feel breathless?"
"Yes."
"What makes it worse?"
"Lying down flat."
"What makes it better?"
"When I sit up."
"Do you have a cough?"
"Yes."
"Do you bring up any spit?"
"Yes."
"What color is it?"
"Pink."

The curtains were drawn round one of the beds on Ward D9. Alec and I had been sent up to take the patient down to X-ray but the house physician hadn't finished yet. So here we were sitting on our trolley like a couple of spare parts while the sluicing and feeding and washing and charting business of the ward went on around us. Six floors below us the morning traffic was flogging its way toward the North Circular. The sky was full of snow which seemed, at this altitude, to be falling upward.

You spend half your life as an orderly waiting for other people—waiting for the meal trolley, waiting for patients, waiting for lab specimens. You have to do something to pass the time.

"Something with his breathing," Alec said.

"Heart attack," I told him.

"How do you know?" Alec whispered.

"He complained of chest pain."

"He didn't look like a heart attack."

"What do you say, then?" I said.

"Chronny Bronny."

I shook my head. He was wrong. Most of the chronic bronchitics looked thin and gray with huge veins. This old guy didn't have the right complexion. Also there were no cigarettes in his locker.

"Bet you a quid."

"You're on."

From behind the curtain the catechism continued:

"*How's your appetite?*"

"*Not good.*"

"*Do you have any tummy pain?*"

"*No.*"

"She'll ask whether his bowels are regular," I predicted.

"*Are your bowels regular?*" came the question from the other side of the curtains.

I knew the next one as well: "What color are your motions?"

"*What color are your motions?*" the doctor asked obligingly.

"I never look," the old man said.

Alec leaned toward me in the trolley. "Why do they ask that?"

"White means a gallstone, black means an ulcer."

"Where did you find that out?" Alec said.

"I read it in a textbook."

Alec laughed aloud. He had started life as a fitter on Clydeside and had never adjusted to a quieter environment. "You bloody power."

The curtains opened and the doctor poked her head out. She was about three years younger than I was and her top pocket was full of pens. She looked hot and flustered. "Can we have some *shush,*" she said and closed the curtains again.

In the background I had briefly seen the old man. He had a bluish tinge to his lips. Definitely a heart attack.

Alec made a face. Behind the curtains the clear, juvenile voice resumed:

"How are your waterworks?"

"All right."

"How often do you pass water?"

"Maybe twice a day."

"Do you get up at night?"

"Yes."

"How often?"

"Three times."

It's called the systemic inquiry and it's the checklist that doctors use to assess the state of every system in the body. If you hear it only once it must sound as though they're asking very specific and pertinent questions, but when you've heard it as often as I have you realize it's the same for everyone. You don't have to be a doctor to elicit information. I had more to remember when I worked as a bus conductor. Making sense of the answers is the only difficult part.

"I think you've got heart failure," said the voice on the other side of the curtains. "I'm going to give you an injection; then we'll get an electrocardiogram." She pushed back the curtains and addressed Alec and me. "Forget the X ray; we'll have it done on the ward. He'll need an ECG though."

The doctor hurried off to write up her notes. I held out my hand to Alec. "Pound you owe me."

"She said heart failure, not heart attack."

"I was close," I said.

"Not close enough. Are you going to get the ECG machine?"

"Are you kidding? It's lunchtime."

Alec shook his head. "You're the kind of bloke who gives NUPE a bad name."

That was how it started—as a game we used to enliven the business of portering. There's not much pleasure to be derived from endlessly transferring patients from ward to ward, down in the lift to X-ray or along the interminable creaking corridors to theater. The West Harwood is a fair-sized hospital but after a few months I could find my way around it with my eyes shut.

Whenever I had nothing to do I'd hang around on the wards. The nurses were too busy to worry about me and most of the doctors were grateful for an extra pair of hands. I'd be called on to hold an arm still while they put up a drip or support a patient while they listened to his chest. Over a period of several months I became fairly conversant with the routine if not the purpose of most medical procedures. I watched wounds being sewn, bandages being applied, blood being taken, forms being signed, eyes and ears and throats being examined. Considering the inflated status of these people it seemed ridiculously straightforward.

It gradually dawned on me that the doctors were a pretty ordinary bunch. Most of them were my age and came from the same kind of background. They all assumed that they were cleverer than I was. I suppose my interest in the subject was prompted by a desire to prove them wrong. Now and again I'd volunteer a diagnosis. Now and again I'd be correct and they'd have a good laugh, the way one does at a monkey who's learned to count.

Simon Hennessey was one of the few who took me seriously. I'd helped him once on a resus attempt and he remembered my name ever since. On a couple of occasions since then I'd caught him alone in the dining room and managed to engage him in conversation. He didn't resent my tagging along on the wards and seemed less keen on preserving his mystique than the rest of them. He had a fashionably cynical attitude to the work. I remember him saying once that hospitals saved very few lives, that their main function was to obscure the inevitability of death and that people were happy if something appeared to be being done. Nonetheless he appeared to do it very well. He made it all seem simple.

I envied that—his consummate sense of ease. I envied his conviction. I envied his confidence. I envied his casual silences and ready wit. I envied his power and I envied him his work in which all these things—strength, power, intellect, decisiveness—seemed to fuse. It seemed to me that, if things had gone differently, he was the man I would have been.

The general response to his death was one of incredulity. There was nothing particularly odd about the circumstances—that wet, foggy November motorcycle casualties were commonplace—what shocked everyone was the fact that someone who led such an apparently charmed life could be killed. But when Alec relayed the news to me my first reaction was a *frisson* of anticipation. The feeling of prescience was reinforced that afternoon when Slattery asked me to collect the dead man's belongings and take them to reception.

*   *   *

The doctors' residence, like the rest of the West Harwood, was an architectural interloper. Towering above
the terraced houses, it had the appearance of having
been dropped from the sky into a half-prepared site. I
took a lift to the fifth floor and let myself into flat 504.
The layout of all these flats was the same—small
kitchen, lounge, bathroom and bedroom. The kitchen
was unnaturally tidy. In his bedroom the sheets had been
folded back. I walked through to the lounge and found
his bags—a couple of holdalls, a cardboard box full of
books and a brown leather suitcase with the brass initials
S.G.H.—Simon Garfield Hennessey.
Up until that moment I'd intended simply to collect
his bags and get out, but finding myself alone in the flat
the temptation to rifle through his belongings proved too
much. I tried the brass clasps and the suitcase sprang
open. His shorts and shirts had been carefully folded.
There was a textbook, a stethoscope and a pair of expensive kid shoes tucked down one side. On top of the
clothes were a college tie; some papers and a book of
photographs.
I pocketed the tie, put the papers to one side and
took out the album—a well-thumbed book with an em-
bossed leather cover. Under the flyleaf was a prep-school
photo—rows of scrubbed and uniformed boys with severe haircuts and grown-up expressions on their faces. I
could recognize Simon standing in the back row with the
taller boys—the same quiff of blond hair, the same confident grin. The rest of the photos were in color, arranged in chronological order—the exclusive public
school, the parents' country house and the halcyon university days—a life measured in summer afternoons.
Here he was in his late teens in Venice, his arm around a
dark, laughing girl in a summer frock. Here reading
from a book on the lawn of a Cambridge college, here
with shorter hair, arm in arm with a group of drunken

revelers, and here, dressed as an RAF pilot, in the cast of some university play. His past, that's what I envied more than anything—the green lawns, the river, the picnics, the dances, the wit and erudition and sexual adventuring. That's the past I wanted—Filbourne School and Clare College, Cambridge. An effortless progression to the London teaching hospitals. A clutch of A levels, a scattering of distinctions. I reflected on the erratic progress of my own life, a sorry itinerary of false starts and wrong turnings. In contrast, Simon's had the smooth forward movement of a luxury cruise.

I put the album back on top of his clothes and flicked back through the documents. One was his curriculum vitae, another turned out to be his medical registration certificate. The third was a small pink slip confirming his membership in the Medical Defense Union. Among them were two white envelopes. The one that had been opened was postmarked Bristol. He had received it two days before his death.

> *Department of Accidents and Emergencies*
> *Royal Clifton Hospital*
> *Clifton*
> *Bristol*
>
> *Dear Dr. Hennessey,*
> *Many thanks for your application. Having contacted your referees I am pleased to invite you for an interview sometime before the Christmas break—would 2:30 P.M. on the 17th December be convenient?*
>
> *Yours sincerely,*
> *Dr. B. Mountford MB (Oxon) MRCP (Edin.)*

The sealed envelope contained Simon Hennessey's intended reply.

West Harwood Hospital
West Harwood
London

Dear Dr. Mountford,
Thank you for your letter of 30th November. I apolo-
gize for wasting your time but since applying for the
above position with you I have been invited to take part
in a theatrical production. This has always been a se-
cret passion of mine so I've decided to take a few
months off to pursue it. I would therefore like to with-
draw my application. Many thanks for your kind offer
and I hope that my withdrawal does not cause you too
much inconvenience.

Yours sincerely,
Dr. Simon Hennessey

It was dated two days previously but had never been sent.

I considered the CV, the medical certificates and the job offer, then returned to Simon Hennessey's letter and read it again. I never knew he'd been interested in acting. You can know someone professionally and have no idea of his private life. This thought hummed through me like a chord. If there was anyone I wanted to be it was Simon Hennessey. Now, as if by magic, the opportunity was in my hands.

To exploit it must seem like the act of a lunatic. Well, I wasn't mad. I was desperate. I had grown up with the burden of a promising childhood. Since then, year after year I had watched my contemporaries outstrip me. The doctors I worked with grew younger, as did lawyers, businessmen, film stars and sports personalities. I had stood on the fringes and watched this gaudy caravan pull away from me. It would never slow down but for one brief moment I had the chance to hurl myself on board.

I returned to his suitcase and rifled through it. The

medical textbook was Davidson's *Principles and Practice* but I had a more recent version of my own. I pocketed the stethoscope, the documents, the CV and the letters, then tried on the white kid shoes. They fitted perfectly.

That evening I left the pub at ten and made my way back through the hospital to the surgical secretaries' office. Light from the ENT wards filtered through the venetian blinds and fell on rows of metal shelves. The ranks of typewriters lay idle under their dust covers. I sat in one of the swivel chairs, took out a sheet of hospital notepaper and began, haltingly, to type. After several false starts I managed a clean copy of the following.

> *Dear Dr. Mountford,*
> *Thank you for your letter of 14th November inviting me for an interview. 2:30 P.M. on the 17th of December would be fine. I look forward to meeting you.*
>
> *Yours sincerely,*
> *Simon Hennessey*

CHAPTER
3

THEY WERE SITTING WITH THEIR BACKS to the light. For a few seconds I was blinded and stood there blinking like an idiot. I staggered forward and one of the dark shapes rose to meet me. As he did so his round body obliterated some of the sunshine. I walked toward them. It seemed like miles across that glaring mahogany boardroom, and as I walked my mind was in fast reverse again, trying to remember something, anything of Simon Hennessey's CV. I must have read it a dozen times on the train. It was only three pages long and I could picture every one of them but by now I couldn't recall a word of the bloody thing. And when I sat down with Mountford pumping my sweaty palm and the sunlight roaring off the table I knew for certain that I was lost.

"I'm Dr. Thorn."

Now I was sitting in the shade of the bookcase I was
able to make out the speaker—a face that seemed to have
been carved from rock, from the severe, straight margins
of the jowls to the granite strata of his dark gray hair.
Only his eyes were alive. They were almost obscured by
the chiseled bags beneath them and the heavy brows
above but in these small slits one sensed constant vig-
ilance—like the apertures of gun emplacements. In seven
months I never once saw him blink.

Mountford couldn't have been more different. He
was about sixty, several years older than Thorn, fat and
jovial, balding and benign. If anything, Mountford made
things worse because he talked so much. Thorn was the
murderer in the fairground and every time that I looked
away from Mountford—talking, rustling papers, blowing
his nose or dabbing at his happy pink eyes with his silk
Paisley-pattern handkerchief, I'd see Thorn giving me a
baleful stare or picking his nails or drumming impatiently
on the table. Listening, waiting.

So there we sat—the three of us: Mountford flicking
through Hennessey's CV, saying "Yes yes yes" and "Very
good, excellent." I'd have given anything to see what he
was reading. I still couldn't remember a word of it. At
intervals Mountford read details aloud. I'd known them
once but now they sounded as random and unfamiliar as
names in a lottery:

"Graduated from Addenbrookes . . . house jobs, Dr.
Ward and Dr. Myers . . . transplant unit, yes . . . SHO.
Ah yes. Oh then general medicine at the Ham-
mersmith . . ." He slid it over to Dr. Thorn and smiled
over the half-moon spectacles at me. As he rambled on I
was aware of Thorn thumbing the pages and scrutinizing
his own fingers. Mountford had taken off his glasses and
was polishing the lenses, still beaming vaguely in my direction.

"So," he said, suddenly replacing them. "Tell us
about Cambridge."

I hesitated. In the wake of Mountford's question all I could hear was the tiny, distant scream of a central-heating radiator. Mountford himself stepped into the gap. "I'm an Oxford man but I know a lot of the chaps. Is old Professor Simpson still there?" he asked.

"Oh . . . ah . . . yes."

"And old Pearson?" Mountford continued happily.

"That's right."

". . . or has he retired now?"

"I think he's retired," I said wildly. I'd clamped a hand on each thigh and could feel the moisture soaking through my trousers. Ironically, the old fool was only trying to put me at ease.

Thorn, expressionless, said to me, "Actually Clive Pearson died the last year you were there."

Another screaming silence.

"I didn't know that." Mountford looked at Thorn and then, accusingly, at me.

"I forgot . . . sorry." I could feel the blood surging into my face.

Thorn's eyes hadn't left me. "Don't get yourself in a paddy," he advised without sympathy. "We're not trying to catch you out . . . not yet." He speared Hennessey's CV with a bony finger. "This is a very good résumé . . . honors physiology . . . high-flying surgical job . . . liver transplants . . . could take you almost anywhere . . . what I want to know is why you decided to come here."

"I liked the idea of working in casualty," I said.

"Did you apply for any other casualty jobs?"

"Yes."

"Any others in Bristol?"

"Yes."

"Did you apply for the Cabot West job?"

"Yes," I said, hurling myself into his trap in a frenzy of sincerity.

"I'm on the board of Cabot West," he said. "I don't remember your application."

"Probably got lost in the post," Mountford volunteered, chuckling.

"Probably," said Thorn.

The red-leather seat cover creaked underneath me. Thorn leaned toward me over the table. There were about three feet of polished wood separating us but I felt as though he was breathing in my face.

"The truth of it is this," he said. "You undoubtedly have the best academic record of the applicants we've seen . . . on paper. But, as you know, any fool can look good on paper."

Mountford giggled at this. Thorn continued evenly, "To be frank, I'm not interested in qualifications. All I need to know is that you genuinely want the job, that you won't find something you prefer and let us down at the last moment."

For a second I wondered if he knew the true story. Of course he didn't, he couldn't, but I should have taken note then of the man's uncanny powers of perception. Studying his face I noted, for all its deep trenches, no smile lines around the eyes or mouth.

"I do want the job," I said. "And I've got no other irons in the fire."

"Isn't that rather risky?"

"To tell the truth, I'd been thinking of taking a few months out."

"May I ask why?"

"I was going to appear in a play. I do a bit of acting. It's just a hobby."

Mountford went "Aha" and looked encouraging.

Thorn said, "I can't see that doing your career much good."

"You're right," I said. "It would have been a mistake."

"So you applied for this job as a stopgap?"

"Yes," I said, still looking at him, almost convinced myself by this inversion of the truth.

Thorn sighed and leaned back in his chair. "Well," he said, "at least you're honest."

They told me to wait outside so I hung around in the paneled corridor outside.

Beyond the doors I could hear the voices of my inquisitors. Mountford seemed to be doing most of the talking. I unwrapped another piece of chewing gum and managed to get it into my mouth without dropping it. I felt physically exhausted. I was pretty sure I'd blown the interview but I congratulated myself on having survived it. After a lifetime of failure you learn to take pride even in qualified success. Outside I could see Brunel's suspension bridge—a filigree of white steel strung across the Gorge.

The door opened behind me. It was Thorn. "Dr. Hennessey?" he said, and somewhere in his funereal tone there was a faint ring of welcome. Behind him I saw Mountford coming toward me, chuckling and holding out his chubby hand.

I moved forward in a daze. The heavy doors closed behind me. I was in.

CHAPTER
4

17th Dec.

Dear J,
It's been snowing since Friday and the hospital looks like an exotic Swiss ski resort. I sit in the dining room and watch patients being wheeled in and out of the French windows, tucked up in blankets and staring out over the Gorge.

We just had interviews for the new casualty officer—the usual troop of cocky young recruits. I had the job of escorting them to and from the interview. Bright young hopefuls going in, disappointed faces coming out. The poor little things—the system doesn't prepare them for disappointment.

Anyway, surprise surprise, they gave the job to a

*rank outsider called Simon Hennessey—seemed a bit
more interesting than the rest of them—quite attractive
in a haunted sort of way. He looked positively sick with
nerves when he went in but Mountford apparently
liked him. Heaven only knows we need some new blood
here. Most of the other doctors are a bunch of over-
confident bottom-pinchers.*

*I'm on earlies these days so I go down to the Wa-
tershed and have a drink with the usual crowd in a bar
overlooking the harbor and maybe see a film, then
wander home and go to sleep on my own. I know I
should fraternize more with the hospital people but
honestly it would kill me. I'm being very good, you'd be
proud of me.*

Take care, see you soon.

Love,
Christine

CHAPTER
5

I LEFT THE ROYAL CLIFTON HOSPITAL on the run.
Sometimes you get so tightly wound that physical exer-
tion is the only release. I ran out through the main door
with my heavy coat flapping behind me. The driveway
curved upward through a snow-covered lawn. The gut-
ters were running with melted snow and the pavement
was booby-trapped with scabs of half-thawed ice. I made
it onto the main road where big detached houses were
lurking behind the trees, then I carried on down the shallow sweeping curve toward the suspension bridge.

I paid at the tollbooth and walked out into space.
Two hundred feet below me the water of the Avon spar-
kled like mica. From the middle of the bridge I looked
back at the Royal Clifton Hospital draped in snow and
foliage on the near side of the Gorge. A covered walkway

ran along the first floor and around to the terraced gardens at the south side. None of the extensions and service buildings that marred the rear of the hospital could be seen from here—just two stories of Palladian windows, the walkway and the intricate roof. I'd been an orderly at the West Harwood for eighteen months, but this place bore no comparison. It didn't look like a hospital at all. It looked like a palace. I buttoned my coat up to the neck and continued across the bridge, then down through Clifton toward Temple Meads station.

The high-speed train from Bristol to London takes an hour and forty minutes to cross the country. The tube from Paddington station to the West Harwood Hospital takes less than half as long but you feel you have traversed a continent. Most people think of London as Tower Bridge or the Houses of Parliament or that chain of parks between Notting Hill and Westminster. Or those chintzy little streets round Chelsea full of boutiques and wine bars. Or those places along the river at Chiswick with windows like beer bottles. Or Piccadilly Circus. Or the West End. That's not London, that's just the old tart's makeup. If you want to know London, the real London, drive two miles from the center of town in any direction. That's my London—the rows and rows of discount stores. The drab, dreary shopfronts caked with exhaust smoke and shaken to their roots with heavy traffic. And beyond the landscape of despair—street upon nameless street of dingy terraced housing—even on the tube it takes you an hour to get clear of it—and if you've lived there all your life—as I have, it can take years. It's a terrifically difficult place to escape from—I can't explain this. It's as if London, by virtue of its size, exerts a sort of gravitational pull. The only people I know who've escaped have done so by moving very rapidly to a place far outside its orbit. Like my sister, Jackie, who became a hotel manager and went to Hong Kong, or my schoolfriends Barry and Shugs, who joined the army.

The other way out I guess is feet first, my father's chosen exit.

My mother has never achieved escape velocity. She has no desire to. She was always quite happy with her china shop, selling vases and trinkets to the tourists on Portobello Road. As far as I know she's still at it. We've never been close. She has always found it difficult to disguise her disappointment in me.

From the station it was a further fifteen minutes' walk to the hospital through those nameless ranks of yellow-brick houses. The area had nothing to distinguish it: a launderette, a couple of off-licenses. If I'd had any lingering doubts about the wisdom of jacking it all in they were banished then.

The Duke of Palmerston backed on to the proposed site of the new oncology wing. One of its outer walls was braced against subsidence on huge wooden crutches and the paneled interior was on a slight tilt, which gave one the impression of being on board ship. It was heavily patronized by the West Harwood Hospital staff, who had, by some tacit understanding, divided up the territory according to rank—nurses in the alcoves at the back, lab staff along the bar and doctors round the fire. The orderlies used to congregate round the dart board. We were a motley bunch—Wally the ex-con, George the kid on job creation, Samuel the West Indian and Henry the old Polish immigrant who'd never learned to read and write English. Sure they were a friendly enough bunch but I never felt part of them. I felt that in getting close to them I'd be infected by their hopelessness.

Alec, as usual, was at the center of things, cracking jokes, buying rounds. I'd have liked him more if he hadn't been so deliberately indiscriminate in his choice of company. That evening, more than any previous evening, I felt trapped in the wrong role. That's how I seemed to have spent half my life—hovering between the people I aspired to and the people circumstances forced me to associate with. From the direction of the fire I kept hearing snatches of erudite jokes and witty asides. These were the people I belonged with. Not Alec, not George and Sammy and the rest of them.

When he'd finished his game of 301 Alec came over to where I was standing by the Christmas tree. "Where have you been all day?"

"Day off," I said.

"I know that, where have you been?"

"Bristol."

"Nice there?"

I remembered my walk to the station. At its westernmost border Clifton ends, suspended in midair—a curtain wall of stone and wrought iron, of balconies and lyre-shaped stairways. Seeing this from the suspension bridge I'd imagined it to be no more than an elegant façade but I was wrong. That graceful curve of buildings swept into another crescent and another, continuing down the hill in the lazy concentric sweeps of a falling leaf.

Against the deepening blue of the sky the pale sandstone shone like gold. I found tree-lined squares, balustrades and archways, porches and conservatories, small neat gardens and oddly shaped pubs crammed in the interstices between square and crescent, mews and boulevard. The Georgian symmetry, the circles and crescents, the triangular architraves and ramps gave the whole place the feel of a life-sized Toytown constructed from a rich child's building bricks. I couldn't imagine not being happy there.

"Bristol's fine," I said.

"What were you doing there?" he asked.

"Looking for a job."

"You've already got a job."

"I mean a better job."

"What kind of better job?"

"Crewing on a yacht," I said.

"It's surely not the best time of year for it."

"We don't leave till the first of February."

"Going where, for Christ's sakes?"

I picked a pine needle out of my drink. "The Caribbean. The Turks and Caicos Islands."

I'd seen a documentary about the Turks and Caicos a couple of weeks previously. I remembered a reef, a few scraggy palms and a lot of sand. It seemed like a good place to disappear.

Alec wiped beer off his moustache. "Jees," he said. "What made you apply for that?"

"I need a change—it's got to be better than this."

"You think so? Tying up ropes for a lot of rich prats. You're better off here. At least you're doing something useful."

"Any fool can wheel trolleys about."

"That's not what we're here for. We're a crucial part of the system, Matthew. We inject a bit of humor. A bit of goodwill. You can't put a price on that."

"Don't you have any ambition?"

He stuck out his lower lip. "Can't say I've ever felt the need for it."

That was where we were different. He was content to be a cog in the machine. There are a hundred ways of justifying being the underdog and the Scottish working class is master of all of them. If it's all you ever knew you can probably convince yourself of the dignity of labor and all that bullshit but I hadn't always lived in the swamp. I knew it got better higher up.

Alec tapped my glass. "Come on with you. I'll buy you another."

"Thanks," I said, "but it's a bit stifling in here. I'm getting out."

CHAPTER
6

I GAVE SLATTERY, THE HEAD ORDERLY, a month's notice.
I'd have preferred just to drop him in it but Alec forced
me to tell him. Our friendship, such as it was, was constantly jeopardized by his outdated code of honor. Over
the next fortnight Slattery took every opportunity to needle me. He developed a rather repetitive homily on the
inconstancy of youth. Youth? Ha! I was twenty-seven. I'd
wasted far too much time already. Slattery's best line was
that I'd never work as an orderly again. I had to laugh at
this as I closed the door of the orderlies' room, leaving
him wheezing with rage in the yellow fog of his own cigarette smoke.

In my last four weeks I seized every opportunity to
spend time on the wards. Most evenings I locked myself
in my bedroom with my lists and my textbooks. Strange,

at Manchester I'd been a terrible student. I could never
concentrate on scientific texts—my mind kept jumping
the tracks. I used to cover up with elaborate lies and cha-
rades, then play the fool in tutorials to cover my ignorance. This stratagem worked reasonably well up until
the first-year exams. I went home weighed down with a
sense of disillusionment which matured in those idle summer months into a clinical depression. I never went back
for the resits. I'd decided I was unteachable.

But now, sitting hunched over the textbooks till one
or two in the morning, I felt fired with a mania for
knowledge. I took the lists down every night before I
went to bed. The wallpaper came off in fine strips until
by the beginning of January the wall above my desk had
begun to look as though some wild animal had been tearing at it.

Of course a lot of what I read didn't make any sense
to me but I plowed on through it. Odd words resonated,
odd phrases fell into place. I didn't know how much I'd
remember of it but I didn't much care. There was no
exam to sit. I merely required a stock of technical-sound-
ing words. I had always been impressed by the re-
petitiveness of medical practice. Ulcers, gallstones,
bronchitis and heart attacks—these were the stock-in-
trade and I already knew how to spot them.

I would read until I fell asleep and the sleep that
followed was like the light sleep of heroin—crammed
with happy fantasies—me in a white coat with the collar
up. Me feeling somebody's stomach and gazing into the
middle distance. Me driving a sports car round the noble
castle that was Clifton and up and out into the green
bursting countryside and the sunny, moneyed world of
privilege with the nurse called Christine in a summer
frock and both arms round my neck. Ha-ha.

You think this sounds adolescent, but what's adolescence? It's the period of your life when you're least cir-
cuitous about your desires. We all want sex, fame and

money. Before adolescence you're too young to identify it and afterward you're too scared of not getting it. It's only in adolescence that you declare these things, that the pocked and pimpled surface of your soul is truly visible. I'm one of the few adults who have tried to make it happen. I'm one of the few honest ones and I'm a bloody imposter.

On the wards I continued to eavesdrop on the systemic inquiry. Whenever possible I'd insinuate my way behind the curtain and watch the process of physical examination. Christmas and New Year broke over the hospital and washed through it. I was hardly aware of either of them. Alec tried on a couple of occasions to encourage me to socialize. For all his cheery bluster he was a sensitive soul. I think he thought I was cracking up.

The converse was true. I'd never felt more contented.

On the twenty-ninth I went through all my possessions, discarding anything that bore the name Matthew Harris—library card, odd clothes, a few books, a tankard, a couple of towels. There was a gold cigarette case with my name engraved on the inside which I couldn't quite bring myself to part with till the very last. I sealed my passport, birth certificate and driver's license in a manila envelope and packed it in my suitcase. Simon's tie and his old school photograph went on top.

I went to the bank and paid off my overdraft with my last pay check. I'd like to have left owing them money but I didn't want anyone to start looking for me.

I found Alec swimming lengths in the hospital pool. Even in winter they kept the water close to body temperature for the physio patients. Alec went there three or four times a week and religiously swam thirty lengths. The ob-

ject of this exercise was to lose weight—an ambition
never realized due to his rather more frequent visits to
the Palmerston.

I squatted on the edge at the shallow end and waited
for him to return. He swam up, breathing heavily, and
pushed his goggles on to his forehead.

"This is it then, pal?"

"Yep," I said.

We shook hands. "See you again then maybe."

"Maybe."

"Leave me an address where I can write to you."

"I didn't know you could write, Alec."

He splashed some water at me and flopped back into
the pool. "Take care," he said and swam off.

I almost left without leaving him a note but, again, I
didn't want him making inquiries, so I sat on a bench in
the changing room and wrote, "Matthew Harris, % Poste
restante. Grand Turk. Turks and Caicos Islands." The island's postmaster had featured briefly on the documentary, smoking a huge joint in the barren stretch of land
behind his house. If there was a poste restante on the
island that was probably it. I folded the address carefully
and put it in his pocket, which made me briefly feel
rather mean, as though I'd knowingly passed him a dud
check. To salve my conscience I left him my gold cigarette case. I couldn't have kept it anyway.

I took the tube to Paddington and was on the Bristol
train with half an hour to spare. As we pulled out of the
station the sun had come out, the rain had washed the
houses and pavements clean and the whole primeval
jungle was steaming in the weak January sunlight. Out
through Slough with the train gathering speed, whipping
me westward into the fresh green countryside and out of

the black smoking clutches of London. I knew I'd finally made it, that I was leaving for good. I was high on anticipation, alternatively smiling uncontrollably and shivering with fear. I couldn't read. I watched the scenery go by. I went to the bar and got a drink to calm my nerves. I wandered up and down the train. I went to the loo, filled the basin and washed my head and face.

I took my watch off for this and laid it by the side of the basin. It was given to me for my sixteenth birthday and was about the only thing I ever got from my family I ever treasured. It had fine black hands and Roman numerals. Over the years the leather strap had become worn and burnished. I was hardly ever without it. On the back of it was the inscription "To Matthew, love Mum and Dad" with the date.

I opened the window and flung it into the slipstream. It whisked off down the side of the train where I imagine it got mangled up in the wheels. So it was that I got rid of the last tangible vestige of my old life and committed the first act of vandalism of my new one.

CHAPTER
7

Dear J,
Thanks for the book, it was the only good thing about
my birthday. Do you remember last year, holed up in
Charlie's house on the fens loafing around in front of
the fire, drinking mulled wine and listening to the
wind howling over from Siberia. It seems like forever
ago. I spent the night on duty dealing with tired old
drunks and car smashes.

Sometimes, in the dark night of the soul, I wonder
why I do this job. Why does anybody do this job? It's
physically exhausting, emotionally draining, no money,
no status. Sometimes you wonder if you're driven less
by compassion than by masochism. Thinking about this,
I remembered how, in the convent, they'd make us say
the Credo each morning with our arms held out to ei-

ther side. And if your arms dropped you didn't love God enough. It was the same equation then: either suffer the pain or suffer the guilt. I suffered the pain. The guilt would have been far worse. I think the same applies now. But occasionally I still miss the good times.

Maybe when that neurotic doctor starts, things will get a bit more crazy. Meanwhile I go to the Arnolfini and talk to the cat. You'd love my house. I live on the corner of the Paragon. It feels like the top of the world. On one side I can see the whole of Bristol and on the other I can see the bridge. In summer I'll open all the windows and let the wind blow through it. Right now is still too cold.

Wrap up tight yourself. You can't be too careful at your age.

I'll see you this weekend.

All my love,
Christine

CHAPTER
8

NIGHT WAS FALLING AS THE TRAIN reached Bristol. It was a wet Friday evening and Temple Meads station was full of commuters. I took a taxi back through the town. In a month the place had changed subtly—there were long queues at the bus stops and the bars on Park Street were full of office workers. Driving up through Clifton we passed groups of students walking home from the university.

The taxi stopped at the tollgate before the bridge and I saw the hospital. Its lighted windows flickered behind the moving trees and the sky behind it was alive with clouds. An ambulance came up behind us and pursued us across the bridge. At the far side we pulled over to let it pass and it hurried on toward the Accident Department, the silent beacon staining the wet road blue.

We turned off from the main hospital driveway and followed the signs to the doctors' residence. It turned out to be a large detached house built at the north side of the hospital and forming with it two sides of a walled orchard. I paid the taxi driver, unloaded my suitcase and stood in the doorway trying to muster courage as he pulled away.

"Hello, stranger."

I turned and saw a large blond woman in a white coat come striding out of the dusk.

"You must be the new cas. officer."

"How did you know?"

"Oh, it's a small world. Word gets around."

This was the last thing I wanted to hear. I looked after the taxi, now rounding the curve of the driveway and melting out of sight.

"I'm Hillary," she told me. "We work back to back. Here, let me take one of these."

She picked up one of my bags and led me into the residence—a scarred wooden hallway with a colonial dinner going at one end. Through an open doorway I could see various characters in white coats drinking beer. Hillary steamed on in this direction. I followed in her wake with my other bags.

"This is Simon Hennessey," she announced. "He's the new cas. officer."

A group of strange faces turned from the bar. Someone bought me a pint and everybody else shook my hand. On the walls there were sports trophies and college ties. They all told me their names, which were Colin and Andrea and others I forget, then went back to talking about paraphimosis and esophagitis and I remembered, as a child, sitting at the dinner table, listening to my father and his partners discussing legal cases in a way that I found equally incomprehensible. I hovered on the edge of the group expressing amazement or amusement wherever it seemed to be appropriate. Hillary told me she was the social secretary and took five pounds off me for the bar subscription. I drained my pint as quickly as possible, picked up my key and retreated.

I'd been allocated a long room at the top of the house with a sloping ceiling and two dormer windows through which I could just make out the lights of the bridge. There was a dressing table, a heavy mahogany wardrobe, and a single bed. I unpacked some of my clothes and hung them up. I took down the calendar (English seaside towns) and replaced it with Simon's school photograph. I moved the dressing table two feet to one side so that it wouldn't obscure the window and I hung around for another hour listening to the occasional peals of laughter from the bar downstairs and occasionally glancing at my wrist where, of course, I no longer wore a watch. I flicked through a book but was too nervous to read so I put on a white coat and began a nighttime tour of the hospital, marking my territory like a dog—through the dining room and out onto the walkway, then back through the administrative section where my interview had taken place. I came out in the central courtyard, where now the black surface of the tennis courts reflected the light of a hundred windows. I climbed two floors and looked in on the wards, then wandered down to the Accident Department at the rear of the hospital where I found a very sleek, very young doctor reducing a fractured wrist.

"Ah, great! Assistance. You must be the Orthopod."

"No, I'm Matth . . . Simon Hennessey, the new cas. officer."

"Whatever. We need a bit of help here. Nurse hasn't had her Weetabix. Hang on this arm."

I held the old patient's anesthetized arm just above the blood-pressure cuff. The doctor gave a pull on the lower arm and we all felt the bones click back into place.

"There, simple, thanks."

"No problem," I said and left. Ha-ha. Fixing broken

arms—all in a day's work. I carried on through the hospital, relishing the swish and crackle of my clean white coat and the clipped sound of Simon's leather soles on the marble floors. I poked my nose into the medical wards, where one of the nurses asked me to sign some X-ray request forms, then offered me tea and chocolates. You wear a gray orderly's jacket and everyone takes you for granted. You swap it for a white coat and even giving your autograph is regarded as an act of great kindness.

I came out of a side entrance and walked through the labs and outbuildings, across the orchard and into the doctors' residence. They were still carousing in the bar, but I didn't want to push my luck so I went upstairs to bed.

Mountford met me briefly the next morning to explain that there were three shifts in the Accident Department and that I was starting on the afternoon one. Again I tried to look at textbooks but all the knowledge I had assimilated up till then was stacked in my head like a house of cards and the addition of one more unit threatened the whole construction. Instead I went for a walk across the suspension bridge. Some people with ropes were attempting to scale the cliffs below the camera obscura. I watched them clinging to the rock face, hardly seeming to move. They had climbed about a third of the way up the rock face—the point where, simultaneously, confidence evaporates and you discover it is too dangerous to go back.

Back at the doctors' residence I found the door to my room unlocked. Inside the bed had been made, my half-unpacked suitcase had been parked beneath it, the calendar had been replaced on the wall and the dressing table had been pushed back into its original position. I hauled out the suitcase and found to my relief that the contents hadn't been tampered with. The manila envelope was still sealed. I took it out and looked around for somewhere to hide it. I thought for a while of putting it under the carpet, but there was no underlay and every contour of the boards was clearly visible. Apart from that, the room, furnished as it was with farmhouse simplicity, afforded few other hiding places. I eventually decided on the wardrobe. I wrestled it out from the wall and taped my envelope behind it.

Afterward I showered, lounged, paced the room. Time crawled on from ten till half-past, eleven till twelve, then seemed to suddenly gather momentum and the last half hour passed in a blur, picking me up and projecting me into the Casualty Department with my stethoscope clutched in my hand and my heart fluttering in my throat.

The patients sitting on benches in the casualty foyer appraised me as I walked past. There seemed to be a hell of a lot of them. The girl at the reception desk was busy writing a man's particulars in a book. There was a queue of four other people behind him.

I came out of the waiting room and rounded a corner into the Accident Department. On the left was the treatment room where minor operations and plastering took place. Beyond that was the resuscitation room where the dead or dying were rushed—a tiled chamber with a huge X-ray machine suspended from the roof and chrome hardware arranged along the walls. The other side of the hallway was made up of six examination cubicles. Four of these were curtained off and from one of them I could now hear the doctor called Hillary:

"Where's the pain? . . . Where else do you feel it? . . . What makes it better? . . . What makes it worse?"

There was something briefly reassuring about that familiar litany. I walked out of earshot, into the doctors' room, and found Christine.

She was sitting in a chair and bending over to fix her laces—taking off her outdoor shoes and slipping on her nursing shoes. She had very flexible joints so she was bent at right angles with her knees in her armpits and seemed to be able to sustain this position with no apparent effort. When I came in she looked up briefly, pushing her hair out of her eyes.

"You're the new chap," she said. "I'm on with you for this week." Then she went back to tying her shoes. As she stood to button her collar I saw her face again—straight brows and dark serious eyes and a smile as bright and sudden as a neon sign. She moved with the supple carelessness of a Degas ballerina—bending to close her bag with her legs apart and one hand holding her hair back— I found it as provocative as it was unintentional.

"At least you're not too young," she said.

Now she was taking pins out of her mouth and putting them in her hair. She spoke through them. "Most of the ones they send here look just out of shorts. . . . What jobs have you done?"

"This and that."

"I mean, where did you work?"

"Here and there." I said evasively.

"I know," she smiled. "Everybody asks you that. Boring, isn't it? Your mind goes after eight hours here. Did they get you somewhere to stay?"

"I'm in the doctors' residence."

"Met the gnome yet?"

"What gnome?"

"You'll see," she said and smiled.

Hillary came in. She looked exhausted but even portering can do that to you. You sweat so much in the heat you probably lose half a stone each day. You go back to your flat smelling of antibiotics and talcum powder. After a while it changes the smell of your sweat.

"Hello," she said. "There's a kid with something in his eye in Two. There's a drunk with a head injury in One and a lacerated thumb in Three. You've got a first-trimester threatened abortion in Four, and a compound tibia just come into resus."

She handed me a bundle of printed cards and took off her coat.

I looked to Christine for assistance. She was tying on a plastic apron. "I've got a Paracetamol overdose to look after," she said. "I'll bc with you in fifteen minutes."

Hillary picked up her cardigan and left. Christine was already gone. I could hear the voices of a dozen patients filtering through from the waiting room. I'd expected problems but not so many—not all at once. I looked at the row of curtains and then down at the cards in my hand. The top one was number 3. I played them as they were dealt.

CHAPTER
9

"LACERATION TO THUMB" TURNED OUT TO be a teen-
ager with sawdust on his jeans and blood all over his
shirt.

The cut had begun to close but opened as soon as I
touched it—a one-inch clean gash running vertically like
the split skin of an overripe plum.

The previous nurse had left a suture pack on the
trolley beside him. I rolled up my sleeves, trying to remember the components of that swooping and twisting
motion with which Simon had showed me to tie knots. I
took an overlong time washing my hands, and must have
looked worried because he said, "It's not serious, is it?"

"No, we see a lot of these," I replied, ". . . gloves,
gloves." Over the noise of the tap I could hear a young
woman moaning behind the curtain to my left and a

young boy, close to tears, saying, "When's the doctor coming?"

His mother shut the brat up.

I dried my hands. Already my mind was leaping ahead to the four other patients in the cubicles and the dozen waiting outside. Now I could hear someone wailing. I could hear doors opening. I could hear someone retching in the sluice. . . .

I couldn't find the gloves. Where were the bloody gloves? I eventually located them under the dressing pack. There is a way of putting these things on without touching their outer surface but the fluency with which I had seen this performed a hundred times belied a potential nightmare of twisted rubber. I ended up with both hands strangled. When I tore the gloves off one of them fell on the floor.

"Having problems?"

"Bloody things. Sometimes they give you two left hands."

We both laughed without humor. A leak had sprung in my confidence and his was seeping out through the same breach. I was tearing at the complicated folds of the sterile paper package and he was craning his head to see the instruments which clattered out.

"Do I get an injection?"

"Of course," I said impatiently.

Somehow the sterile and nonsterile equipment had become hopelessly muddled. I gave up the charade of hygiene and fiddled around on the trolley's lower shelves looking for a bottle of Lignocaine. Green needle? Blue needle? They were color-coded according to size. The one I chose looked dangerously large.

"Are you going to stick it in?"

"Just relax," I told him.

His hand was shaking more than mine. I grabbed him by the wrist and stuck the needle in. He yelled and snatched it away. The syringe flew onto the floor and the child next door started bawling.

The carpenter and I glowered at each other.

"Have you ever done this before?" he asked.

"You have to expect some pain," I replied.

"What are you going to do now?"

"I'm going to sew up your thumb."

"You've not given the injection yet."

"You're not getting a bloody injection."

Above the screams of the child to my left I could hear the girl with the threatened miscarriage whispering to her husband and realized that all the patients waiting to be seen were privy to my present shambles. I'd used five minutes without even starting. At this rate it would be more than an hour before I began seeing the patients in the waiting room. Everything was rushing out of control. I turned my back on the bleeding thumb and started foraging among the metalware for a pair of needle forceps. I found the damned suture and clipped it in. When I turned again my patient was sitting on the edge of the trolley with rank fear in his eyes.

"This is going to hurt like hell."

"Tough shit." I said this sotto voce but the kid in cubicle 3 picked up on it and renewed his screams. His mother was saying, "There there, he's not talking to you."

"Lie down," I said to the thumb. He was reluctant to obey, but the cold hatred I now felt for him must have transmitted itself through my voice because he lay still enough.

Sweat was running into my eyes. I tried to wipe it away and got blood from my cuff on to the front of my jacket. The thumb was shaking wildly. I knew he'd pull it away as soon as I'd stabbed it. I held his wrist as hard as I could and poised to strike.

Behind me the curtain opened and Christine said, "What are you doing?"

"I'm sewing this lad's thumb."

"There's a bloke in major with his leg hanging off."

"Just one more stitch." I said, trying to hide the gory chaos from her.

"It can wait."

As I followed Christine through to the resuscitation room I saw out of the corner of my eye the receptionist escorting new patients into cubicles 5 and 6. One of them was holding a bloody rag to his head.

In resus there was a pale man in motorcycle leathers lying under the operating lights. Blood was dripping from his shin and congealing in a gelatinous pancake on the floor. I touched his foot gingerly and he yelled in pain.

Christine said, "Maybe we should stop the bleeding."

I picked up a pack of dressings and hesitated, reluctant to press on the hole in his skin.

"Here," said Christine, steering me out of the way. She pressed hard on his groin and the dripping slowed. "Ring Orthopods. Bleep five-four-three. Then get transfusion."

"You call them," I said. "I'd better stay with the patient."

She hesitated, then shrugged and left me pressing on the motorcyclist's groin. I couldn't think of anything else to do so I asked him some questions about his bowels. As I waited, I pictured the swelling ranks in the waiting room and wondered how long my incompetence could be ignored. Two hours? Three? Christine surely wouldn't let me cock things up for longer than that. What would she do? Phone Thorn, call another doctor, or just let me dig my own grave and see how deep I went?

"Sign this." Christine came back and handed me an X-ray form.

In my confusion I signed it "Matthew Harris" but the signature was so manic that it must have been illegible.

"If it's OK I'll take over here. You've got quite a lot on your plate." She said it with no apparent malice but I was beginning to hate her for her coolness. I did what she suggested. As the orthopedic surgeons wheeled the motorcyclist off to theater I was trying to get near the three-year-old who was now shrieking like a frenzied animal. A chorus of wailing infants echoed him from the waiting room.

With the help of his mother I prized the little fist away from his eyes and tried to separate the lids. There was still blood on my finger and thumb but I was already past caring about such details. The only way I could salvage anything was to see people quickly and get them out of the department. The eye remained limpet tight. The child was choking on his own sobs and the mother was beginning to cry.

"We'll leave him to settle down," I said.

When I turned I found Christine was standing behind me with a small plastic vial in her hand.

"Try some of this."

"What is it?"

"Amethocaine."

"You do it," I said, handing it back. At the time I felt like shoving it down her throat. My hatred for the patients had spread to encompass all humanity.

You think life can get no worse and it does. You reel like a boxer from calamity to calamity, a furious carnival of sweat and blood and screaming. You long for oblivion, which never comes. It is said that terror quickly exhausts itself but I suspect from that terrible afternoon that that particular emotion can sustain itself for many hours longer than most of us like to imagine.

At times I caught a glimpse of myself in a mirror above a washbasin or in the glass of the instrument cabinet door. I saw a man with wild hair and flapping shirt tails, a man streaked with blood and plaster, a man with pens and equipment falling from his pockets. A clown. A doll.

I became obsessed with time, longing for its passage and resenting every tiny distraction which drew me from my task. After each whirlwind consultation Christine would offer a card and I would write on it the ideas of a child in the handwriting of an epileptic: "Came with headache, went home." "Leg. Go to bed." "Stomach. Sick. Go GP tomorrow."

For the last half hour of my shift I sat at the desk in the doctors' room, no longer daring to go out, dripping coffee on my white coat and listening to Christine dealing with the wounded. I was incapable. I couldn't lift the coffee cup without spilling it, nor swallow when I got it to my lips.

At last the doctor on the evening shift took over—the irritatingly confident youth I'd helped with the broken arm. He went to work, Christine went home, and I stayed in the department for another hour trying to make sense of the scribbled cards I'd written and tidy them up a bit. It was a futile gesture made doubly humiliating by this glossy-haired prodigy who'd come in now and again, whistling blithely, and deposit his notes in the out tray. I glanced at one or two of them for inspiration but found only initials and hieroglyphics, the significance of which escaped me, for example:

> P.C: Sudden L.O.C. while out walking
> O/E   C.V.:p'O reg. B.P. 120/80 H.S1 + 11 +
>   0
>   Resp: T O PN Res BS vesic + 0
>   G.I.: Soft O palp OLOKOKOS
>   Neuro Confused, dim P + TR arm
>   Reflexes + + throughout
>   cranials 11 − X11 intact
> Ix   FBC. U+E's + G1
> D: C.V.A.
> Rx   Ref Med reg.

I kept this to look at again because its components appeared on many of his notes and I was sure that, given a bit of time, I could crack the code. The problem remained of what to do with the shabby cards I had produced during my own shift. I'd written so many during those frantic eight hours that it would take me all night to rewrite them. So I left them there—documentary evidence of my incompetence, and walked gloomily back through the hospital.

I'd forgotten in the tropical heat of the Casualty Department how bitterly cold the weather still was outside. I hurried back through the bare orchard and let myself in with the old latchkey. Upstairs I ran a bath and lay in it till the water grew cold. Then I sat in front of the window watching the long thin limbs of the cherry trees rasp against each other in the breeze. The horrible finality of my actions was weighing on me like an illness. I couldn't run away because the first thing they'd do would be to contact the West Harwood in London and ask Personnel for Dr. Hennessey's likely whereabouts. They'd find he'd died some weeks earlier and the hunt for the imposter would be on. Even the most flat-footed detective would surely make the connection with the West Harwood orderly who'd recently resigned. I know it must seem incredible but this was the first time I'd thought this through. There was no escape.

Below my window other white-coated figures were drifting back through the trees toward the residence. I couldn't face the ordeal of talking to any of my new colleagues. I dressed and left the hospital. That evening, leaning on the parapet of Brunel's bridge, I was a whisper away from climbing over and hurling myself into the void. But I didn't. I carried on into Clifton. I found a pub called the Coronation Tap, sat myself at a corner table and drank myself into oblivion.

CHAPTER
10

2nd Feb.

Dear J,
So much for Dr. Hennessey. The others might be pom-
pous twits but at least they know what they are doing. I
can't believe they let people out of medical school like
this. They spend six years filling their heads with scien-
tific theory and they don't have the first idea about first
aid or sterile procedure or normal social behavior for
goodness' sakes. Most nurses could do the job standing
on their heads but instead we have to clear up the mess
and repair the damage for half the pay. I'm sorry, I
know it's a hobbyhorse. I'm sure he'll get better. God
knows he can't get any worse. He reminded me of what

you described as the "breathless intensity" of young ac-
tors who knew their lines but didn't know what the part
was about.

  Enough of that. He'll learn I'm sure.

  How are you, J? Are you still working or are you
resting? Whenever I'm rushing around here like a
blue-arsed fly I think of you sitting in your conservatory restoring the inner man. I'm on for the next
couple of weeks. I really enjoyed seeing you and feeding the ducks in Kensington Gardens. It's funny, isn't
it, how these tiny memories become so important. All the
time I lived in London I never thought twice about our
Sunday morning walks but now I feel very nostalgic
about them.

  Ah me. The virtuous life. Who would have
thought it could be so difficult? You say "follow your
instinct." I just hope it knows where it's going.

  Keep in touch. It's always lovely to hear from you.

All my love,
Christine

CHAPTER
11

I WAS WOKEN BY A MIDGET.

I'd slept badly, surfacing at times to a cold, uncomfortable half-wakefulness, then slipping back until I was finally roused by the sound of a spoon being vigorously stirred in a cup of tea. Sleep slid away and was replaced by a pain like a vise above the bridge of my nose. I belched and turned my head. There was a hand, a cup, and a spoon ladling sugar into it. I don't take sugar.

I looked for the owner of the hand, straining my inflamed eyeballs to the limit of their orbit until, with a start, I saw her. She had a big head, corrugated features, muscular, bowed limbs and hands that seemed to have been inexpertly carved from blocks of wood. I recoiled from her in horror but she must have been used to this because she didn't react.

54

"Not very promising start, eh?" She spoke in a coarse, synthetic contralto over the rattling spoon.

In a nightmare one loses the capacity for surprise. I focused blearily on the housekeeper. She was wearing a child's dress and a pale-blue nylon housecoat. There was a handkerchief tied around her head. I half closed my eyes and willed her to evaporate. Instead she stumped out of sight with her arms held out to either side for balance.

"I just hope you're proud of yourself."

I could hear her doing something to the rug at the foot of my bed. I raised my head and discovered what she was upset about—my shoes lay in the middle of the floor, covered in clods of earth. Their passage across the carpet was clearly marked.

"Leave that, I'll do it."

"There's mud all up them stairs."

"I'm sorry."

"I'm sure you are," she said, still scraping. "There'll be nothing for it but shampoo and water."

"Sorry," I repeated to the wall. I didn't trust myself to rise in case I threw up.

"It's eight o'clock," she said before closing the door. "I like all my doctors up and out by eight-thirty so's I can get on with my business."

Obscene dwarfish insults rose in my throat and I swallowed them. My instinct for self-preservation hadn't entirely abandoned me.

"I'll be up in a minute."

I waited for her to close the door before raising my head off the pillow. I was lying fully clothed on the made-up bed. The legs of my trousers were rucked uncomfortably around my knees. I managed to pull them off, then nausea and fatigue overcame me and I slumped back.

I must have fallen asleep again because the next time I looked at the clock it was nine o'clock. A bucket and scrubbing brush were set in the middle of the floor where

presumably Molly had left them. The phone was ringing.
I raised myself on one elbow and fumbled for the receiver.

"Dr. Hennessey?"

"Speaking."

"This is Dr. Mountford."

"Hello, Dr. Mountford." I was suddenly wide awake
but my tongue was still thick and my voice was hoarse.

"Can I see you please? I'm in the dining room."

There could be only one reason for his call. In a moment I was groping for my towel, oblivious to my physical
symptoms. The headache caught up with me as I blundered across the landing and the nausea as I got to the
bathroom. I knelt on the floor, hugging the lavatory
bowl, and was sick. I could hear Molly clattering about in
a neighboring room. She obviously heard me spewing because she came to the door and called, "Are you all right
in there?"

"Never better," I croaked between convulsions.

Afterward I felt well enough to stand in front of the
mirror and rinse my soiled mouth with water. I found a
dusty bottle of Paracetamols in the bathroom cabinet and
ate four of them. Flecks of blood were floating in the lavatory bowl and the lining of my stomach felt as though it
had been stripped with a blowtorch. I shaved and made it
back to the bedroom. As I leaned against the door I could
hear Molly in the bathroom repeatedly flushing the loo.

I dressed, trying to bend as little as possible. Cold
sweat kept springing from my face. I knew Mountford
was on to me. I was hardly in good enough shape to
reach the dining room, far less to stand up to questioning, but what else could I do? The only option open to
me was to carry the charade through to its conclusion. I
wondered as I made my way between the barren cherry
trees toward the back entrance what they could do to me.
I hadn't put anyone's life at risk. At least I didn't think I
had.

They had been frying bacon in the dining room and the lingering smell almost turned my stomach. Most of the tables had been cleared away and the women behind the servery were having their own coffee. Mountford, in a pinstriped shirt and cravat, was sitting next to the windows that looked out over the hospital's central courtyard. He was reading the foreign pages of the *Telegraph* with a fixedly whimsical expression which may have been a function of his eyesight. I was almost by his table when he noticed me. I must have looked dreadful but he said, "Ah, Hennessey, you look well," as he bounded to his feet and positioned a chair for me.

I knew he was preparing me for the crunch. I sat, hardly breathing, as he carefully folded the paper.

"Would you like a tea, coffee?"

"No, thanks. I've had breakfast."

Mountford laughed at this and smoothed the side of his head. What remained of his hair was thick enough to form small tufts over the legs of his spectacles.

"So," he said taking them off and polishing them furiously, ". . . so how are you settling in?"

"It's all rather unfamiliar," I said. "Everything was a bit chaotic."

"Yes, well, new hospital and so on. Molly looking after you, is she?"

"Yes, thank you." I could feel something solid at the back of my tongue. I swallowed but it didn't go away.

"And the work?"

He was still smiling. I wondered if he was being deliberately disingenuous.

I said, "The turnover of patients is quicker than what I'm used to."

"I'm sure it is, yes, yes. I'm sure it is . . . still . . ."

"I've been thinking about some of the patients I saw yesterday. You may have felt some of my decisions . . ."

"No," said Mountford. "No, no, not at all . . . wouldn't dream of interfering."

I began to suspect that, incredibly, miraculously, Christine hadn't reported my incompetence.

"That middle-aged woman," I said, "with the bad chest . . ."

"Yes?" He was chewing his spectacle leg in a pantomime of concerned concentration. He obviously had no idea who I was talking about. "Yes, what about her?"

"No, nothing."

"If there's anything I can do to help . . ."

"No, it was nothing I couldn't deal with."

"Good."

A bolus of gas erupted from the ferment in my stomach and I tasted the first dangerous traces of sweet saliva. I covered my mouth with my hand. I had to get out of here but Mountford was settling down to his theme: ". . . man of your abilities . . . good to have you on board . . . think of ourselves as a team . . . always like to feel available . . . don't hesitate to . . ."

He had put his spectacles back on. Outside the winter sky was bright as steel. It reflected in his lenses as he turned toward the window, making him look blind and rather stupid.

I took advantage of the hiatus to say, "If you'll excuse me, I've got a couple of things to look after."

"Yes, yes, quite, of course, sorry, you're a busy man."

I stood up and waited for my intestines to catch up with me.

"Anyway," he was saying, "do call in on me anytime. I've enjoyed our little chat."

I nodded, edging round the table.

"I always feel there should be more . . . ho-ho . . . intercourse in the department. You know, Celia and I like to get to know everyone socially . . . in fact . . ."

A new thought had struck him. Now he was fishing for his wallet. My heart sank. Quite apart from my physical distress, I had the idea that the longer I spent in his company the more likely he was to penetrate my disguise.

Mountford was looking through his diary. "Yes, now
. . . where are we? December? No. January . . . ah February . . . March? Let's see. When would you like to have
dinner with Mrs. Mountford and myself? Thursday the
fourteenth would suit us."

"Fine."

"Or the following Wednesday?"

"Anytime," I said desperately.

"Good. The fourteenth then. Now do you want us to
pick you up?"

"No. I'll make my own way, thank you."

"I'd better give you the address then." He started
rummaging in his wallet for a card, gave up looking and
took out his pen. I watched as he wrote his address in
longhand on the back of a napkin. He wrote very slowly.
My stomach heaved.

"There you are."

I nodded, not daring to talk, and backed away.

"Oh, one other thing."

"Mm?"

"Dr. Thorn wanted to see you after his ward round.
He'll probably be back in his office."

I turned away from him so quickly that I hardly
caught his expression when he said this but it seemed, as
I bent, drooling and panting in one of the staff toilets,
that he had been smiling. I was half convinced as I
cleaned myself up with a paper towel that Thorn also
wanted to spend twenty minutes welcoming me into the
fold. That notion was annihilated as soon as I reached his
room.

Thorn's room faced west. It seemed rather small, partly
because of the gloom and partly because of the bulk of
files and books and scientific papers that filled every available space on the shelves and on his desk.

I found him sitting behind the stacked wire trays dictating the morning's discharge letters into a cassette recorder. He was in his shirt sleeves with his white coat hung on a peg behind him. His forearms, covered in white fleece, were planted on either side of the Dictaphone. He allowed me to stand, waiting, while he finished, then he looked up and switched the machine off. The vertical folds on either side of his mouth were cast in iron.

"Sit down."

I sat. Inside his room it must have been the same temperature as the corridor but I felt I was sealing myself in a fridge. I had already noticed the pile of casualty cards at the side of his desk. He now picked these up and began to shuffle through them.

"I'm told," he said, "that you can tell a man's personality from his handwriting. If this is true I would say that you were slovenly, that you were untidy, that you were lazy and that you had no training in any academic discipline, least of all medicine."

I began to speak but he continued as if he hadn't heard me.

"I've had a very large number of junior doctors work for me. My first impressions of them are not always vindicated. But they usually are. My first impression of you is not good. In fact I cannot remember being less impressed by anyone. I find it difficult to imagine that you got away with this standard of care at the West Harwood. There are two possibilities. Either you are not the practitioner your CV suggests you are. Or you are simply not interested in the work here."

"Well, all I can . . ."

He continued to ignore me, reading aloud from the card he had most recently turned up.

"Head injury, aged fourteen. It says here. 'Blow on head, felt sick, slight bruise. OK.'"

He waited for some comment on this. My mind was racing frantically but I could think of nothing to offer.

"Do you mind telling us *where* on his skull he sustained this injury? Do you mind telling us *how* he sustained it . . . or whether he was knocked out?"

"I don't remember."

"And if the ambulance should bring his corpse back the next morning, the boy having died from an extradural hemorrhage, what will you tell his mother then? Will you tell *her* you can't remember him?"

"I don't think he was knocked out."

"You don't appear to think. What's this rubbish?" He got up and started pacing backward and forward behind the desk, too agitated to sit, leafing through the casualty cards, glaring at them, then, glaring at me. "'Small graze on arm, treated with iodine.' Tetanus," he said. "Have you ever heard of tetanus, Dr. Hennessey?"

"Yes."

"And how do we protect against tetanus?"

"They get a jab . . . an injection."

"A vaccination . . . point five of a mill. of antitetanus toxoid intramuscularly and we write it on the card. But I suppose you were too busy—too preoccupied with higher thoughts to bother about the possibility of tetanus."

"I forgot."

"I know bloody well you forgot. You also forgot that this young lady, aged twenty-six, was quite possibly pregnant and yet you saw fit to send her for an abdominal X ray."

"She wasn't pregnant."

"Did you ask her? Do you even know who I'm talking about?"

"Yes," I lied.

He swept past the desk again. His elbow caught a textbook and it crashed to the floor. He thrust the card in front of me. "Well, show me where it is written that she is not pregnant."

"It's not written," I said without looking.

"Exactly," he bellowed. "It is not written down. Nothing's written down. The most you could manage for these people is a few fatuous comments. Did you examine them? Well, did you?"

I nodded.

His face was a weapon—hair and eyebrows projecting in every direction. He turned away from me in disgust and walked to the window where he stood for a while looking westward through the pines to Ashton Court. I felt my stomach contract and the sweat spring from my face again. He turned, more composed now, but still transfixing me with his stare, sharpening every syllable he spoke to a fine point.

"Quite frankly, if not for Dr. Mountford, I wouldn't have hired you, Hennessey. You're either committed to the job or you're not. It's not something you can do at half-cock. Everyone gets a full examination here and everything gets written on the cards. If you find that boring you've no business here. More litigation comes out of here than out of any other hospital department. There's a hundred ways you can kill or maim these patients and somewhere most of them have happened. You put a plater on too tight and the arm withers. You miss an MI and they die on the way home. You don't clean a wound and they come back with gangrene. Do you want me to go on?"

I shook my head.

"Well, just remember this. If you kill someone, and at this rate you almost certainly will, it's your head on the block—not Mountford's, not mine, it's yours. And when the DPP is hauling you over the coals he won't give a damn for your dazzling curriculum vitae. He'll want to know that you can take a history, that you can examine patients properly, that you're capable of applying the basic principles of medical care."

He waited while this sank in, then he slowly bent to pick up the book that had fallen to the floor. A doubt checked him as he straightened.

"You can take a history?"

"Of course."

"And you can examine a patient?"

"Yes."

Something in the way I answered made him look at me again. He paused and peered at me as though forming an outlandish theory which he himself was unwilling to accept. I prayed that his fury had burned itself out.

He turned away from me, put on his white coat and opened the office door.

I rose shakily to my feet.

"Come on then," he said. "You'd better show me."

There was a general medical ward at the end of the corridor and he headed straight for it without pausing to check that I was following. I was beaten now and ready to confess anything, yet I stuck behind him as if dragged on a leash.

He barged into the ward with the most cursory of nods to the duty sister. As I entered the ward an Asian orderly came out whistling. I envied him with all my heart.

Thorn made straight for the center bed.

"This is Dr. Hennessey. He wants to have a look at you. Dr. Hennessey—this is Mr. Weatherilt."

The old man showed me his yellow teeth and put down his newspaper. I couldn't muster a smile to return to him.

"Feel Mr. Weatherilt's pulse," Thorn told me.

I felt it.

"It's irregular," I said.

"It's fast and irregular," said Thorn. ". . . So?"

The medical texts I'd been reading lay submerged in my subconscious but, as I stood, gasping like a drowned fish, a fragment of print floated to the surface.

"He's in atrial fibrillation," I said.

Thorn only grunted. "Listen to his chest."

My hands were shaking as I put the stethoscope to my ears. Weatherilt leaned forward without my asking him. He'd obviously been through this many times before. He breathed in and out. I could hear the rushing of the wind in his chest and another noise, like someone faintly crumpling tissue paper. Simon had described this to me once—I knew it meant something. I lunged blindly for a phrase. "Basal crepitations."

I registered I was right only as a man playing Russian roulette registers that he hasn't blown his head off— any transient spasm of relief was quenched by the terror that preceded and the new, more dreadful terror as the barrel spun again.

"Feel his abdomen."

Weatherilt lifted up his pajama top and I put a hand on his swollen, shiny belly.

"Properly, from the left," said Thorn.

I changed places.

"Feel his liver," said Thorn.

I could remember that. I pressed on the right-hand side, up under the ribs.

"Well, what does it feel like?"

"Normal," I said.

"What do you mean, 'normal'? If you can feel it, it's not normal, is it?"

"No."

"What?"

"No," I said more loudly.

"What is it?"

"Abnormal."

"The word is enlarged. It's an enlarged, smooth, nonpulsatile liver. What are the causes?"

"Hepatitis," I said immediately. I knew this because, while I lived in the squat in Camden I'd had hepatitis for two lousy months. It was one of the most miserable times of my life but, standing sweating and shivering in that hospital ward with my stomach rebelling on me and Thorn putting on the screws, I'd gladly have chosen it in preference.

"And?" he was saying. "And?"

I stammered until he supplied the answers himself, pinching his forehead between finger and thumb as though my ignorance caused him physical pain.

"Cirrhosis," he snapped. "The man's got advanced cirrhosis. Look at him—classic—white nails, spider naevi, wasting, wasting . . . what do you think the blood transfusion's for—yes, varices, my God!"

We confronted each other across Mr. Weatherilt's naked chest. Me pale from fear and nausea, Thorn breathing heavily. Weatherilt smiling benignly at us both.

"Who did you say your referees were?"

I couldn't even remember that. Now surely he had to see through me. "Oh, yes, Ward . . . and Myers," he said. "What's wrong?"

"I think I'm going to be sick," I said.

"Sick, what do you mean, sick?"

I turned and fled down the ward, trying to hold back the rising acid tide.

I got to the loo just in time and threw up bile and more bile. As I bent, gasping, my nose running and my eyes streaming, I prepared myself for the coup de grâce.

He'd left the ward when I went back to look for him. I found him in his study looking out of the window with his hands behind his back.

"Have you been drinking?"

"Yes," I replied.

"Were you drunk yesterday when you were supposed to be working?"

"No."

"I don't believe you."

I was too crushed to protest. Thorn looked at me

long and hard as if trying to wrench the confession from me by force of willpower and it dawned on me that an escape route might be presenting itself.

I hung my head and nodded weakly.

"I need hardly remind you," he said, "that being drunk while practicing is one of the few misdemeanors for which I can have you struck off. I assume this kind of thing hasn't happened before?"

I mumbled, "I'm sorry. I'm so sorry."

Thorn pondered for a while then said. "I'm giving you one chance, Hennessey. Just one. If your performance doesn't improve I intend to terminate your contract at the end of the week with a recommendation to the GMC that you be investigated and disciplined accordingly."

I waited for the rest.

"You can go now," he told me.

I walked, still shaking, back to my room and collapsed on the bed. I had to get up again to spew in the sink—now producing only mucus. I drank as much water as my writhing stomach would hold and got back into bed again. A piece of paper had fallen from my pocket onto the floor. I picked it up. It was the completed card I'd copied from the other casualty officer. I squinted at it through half-closed eyes, convinced that this crumpled Rosetta Stone held the key to my problems. My head pounded and my arm ached as I tried for several minutes to focus on the arcane abbreviations, to learn something, anything, which might save me from ultimate disaster. The effort proved too much for me. The card slipped from my fingers and fell to the floor. I left it there.

CHAPTER
12

HOSPITALS CONCEAL NOTHING; THE WHOLE BUILDING is designed to assist the process of scrutiny. Every surface reflects sound and light. Walking into a hospital is like having your senses sharpened—like removing tinted glasses or having wax cleaned from your ears. At the best of times you feel exposed and vulnerable and walking back into the Royal Clifton that afternoon was not the best of times.

I was convinced that everyone had heard of my incompetence—the African cleaning lady who smiled so broadly as she wrung her mop in a contraption attached to the bucket—the two residents who shot me a sideways glance on their way to Radiography. The student nurses reading the menu outside the dining room who giggled as I passed. Even the few patients sitting in the Accidents waiting room seemed to regard me with suspicion and I imagined as I turned past Reception and into the department that they began talking among themselves in hushed voices.

Now I was in the Accident Department and all other considerations were swamped by my apprehension about meeting Christine again. I almost ran into her as I dived for the cover of the doctors' room.

"Steady," she said.

I apologized, flustered.

"Had a good sleep?"

"Yes, thanks."

"You don't look it."

I picked up the blank cards from the box on the desk. "What have we got waiting?"

She took them from me and put them back in the box. "There's no panic," she said. "Sit down. Relax. It's not busy, there's no need to get in a frenzy."

"I'm sorry, I've got a job to do."

"Correct," she said. "Do you want a cup of tea?"

I hesitated, then sat down. "Yes, please."

"Milk?"

"Yes, please."

"Sugar?"

"Yes. I mean no."

She looked at me.

"No," I said.

She handed me the cup and made herself comfortable. "My God, you are in a state."

"Look, yesterday I just got snowed under. It could happen to anyone."

"Sure it could. It was a hectic shift," she said. "I'm on your side, Simon."

It was the first time anyone had used my new Christian name to my face and it jolted me into submission.

"I think we should get to know each other," she said.

"What do you want to know?" I asked warily.

She shrugged. "I don't know—what made you apply to work in Bristol?"

"Seemed like a nice place."

"Do you come from London?"

"Yes. No. The country. Headley Down."

"Make up your mind."

"Headley Down."

"I come from Cheshire—near Manchester," she told me.

"I went to University at M——" I said, then checked myself, realizing how easily I slipped out of Simon's character and into my own.

"I went to university with someone from Manchester."

She laughed. "I'm not surprised, it's a big place."

I was beginning to warm to her. I marveled that this was the same woman I'd hated so passionately the previous evening. We'd never had a chance to sit down and talk then. I listened nervously for the sound of the hordes of Bristol pouring through Reception and into the department but everything seemed quiet.

"So, how are you liking it here?" she asked.

"It's OK."

"You met Molly?"

"Yes."

"She's a bit bossy but she means well."

"I know."

". . . and old Mountford?"

"Yes."

"Mountford's an amiable nincompoop," she said. "Thorn takes a bit of getting used to."

Another pause, longer this time. I wanted to apologize for my incompetence of the night before but apology involved confession and I couldn't have supported that. Instead I retreated, leaning back and trying to adopt one of Simon's relaxed, sprawling postures. In the wooden chair this turned out not to be possible. She put me out of my misery by broaching the subject herself.

"About the job. It's not as simple as it looks."

"I'm sure I'll manage."

"I'm sure you will too, but you mustn't expect to know everything. If there's something you don't know about just tell me or look it up in a book. I won't hold it against you."

"I'll be all right," I said stiffly.

I drank my tea. She drank hers in silence, then said, "A lot of people come here expecting to take control straightaway. They make a mess, then Thorn gets hot under the collar."

I nodded, affecting casual interest, pretending not to understand this reference despite its utter directness.

She regarded me for a while, then said with genuine compassion, "I'm sorry, am I being terribly tactless?"

There was something about the way she said it—something so translucently concerned that I couldn't help but smile and I suddenly found myself laughing and wiping my eyes and saying, "No, no, it's me, I'm sorry, I'm being very stubborn. You're right. Yesterday was a joke. I kept seeing patients I didn't have the first idea about and trying to bluff my way through. Then Thorn got me in his office and disemboweled me. I've been suicidal."

I stopped there, horrified by the extent of this confession and, at the same time, swept through with the sudden catharsis.

"You're not the first," she said.

I picked up a card. "I'd better see this patient," I said.

"You don't know what's wrong with him."

"It says ankle sprain."

"Well, do you know how to treat an ankle sprain?"

"Of course . . . I mean no."

She went to the bookshelves and handed me Apley's *System of Orthopedics*. "It's on page three-o-two."

She left me with the book on my lap. I opened it at the page on ankle sprains and read it in five minutes. Orthopedics is a mechanical specialty. The concepts are no harder to grasp than those encountered in carpentry and central heating. A sprained ankle is a kind of bruise. If you can wiggle it, it's probably not broken and the treatment is an elastic stocking.

I closed the book and went to see my patient, who was a plumber from Cosham. I wiggled his ankle and pressed it on the inside. He was sore over a bone that the book had called the lateral malleolus. Back in the doctors' room I copied this onto the appropriate form and sent him round to radiology.

Christine came back with the X ray.

"NBI," she said.

"What?"

"No bone injury."

I wrote this down and she squinted at it critically. "Right," she said.

"Right what?"

"Right. It was the right side. You have to put which side."

I wrote this also. The card now said: "Inversion injury, right ankle. On examination, bruising and **tender**ness over lateral malleolus, X ray: NBI. Treated with strapping." If Thorn wanted any more he could sing it himself. Christine checked the "GP to review" box and filed it away. It had taken me half an hour but I did the next one in ten minutes without looking at the book.

Over the next few days most of my work consisted of the learning and reiteration of this kind of recipe. Once I'd delivered myself into Christine's hands, she steered me through each new event with patience and tolerance. It amazed me that she never questioned my ignorance until one evening when we were having coffee in the doctors' room and she said, "You went to Cambridge, didn't you?"

"How did you know?"

She shrugged and didn't answer. Instead she said, "I'm surprised you're not different."

"How different?"

"More of a conccited ass like the rest of them. When did you qualify?"

"Three years ago."

She whistled. "You've been qualified three years and you don't know how to treat a sprained ankle?"

I faltered, blushed, searched for an explanation, and finally noticed she was teasing me.

"It's OK," she said. "There's no reason why you should. It's the ones who pretend who annoy me."

The bell rang to let her know that another patient had been checked through Reception. I could hear him— the ubiquitous Celtic boozer singing "Oh Flower of Scotland" at the far end of the department—singing, as Alec used to, with an extra syllable marking the pauses.

She spoke into the intercom, "I'll be right round," then finished her coffee and wiped her mouth with the back of her hand. When she stood up I caught a glimpse of the black top of her stocking before she straightened her dress.

The most important thing that Christine taught me was that ignorance is permissible. If the nurse doesn't know it, there is always a book, there is always a telephone and at the last resort there is always a specialist who presumably has a book and a telephone of his own. Simon was right—the NHS is a giant game of pass the parcel. The relatives panic and pass it to the GP, the GP passes it to the casualty officer. All the cas. officer has to do is send it home or admit it to hospital. You get an instinct as an orderly for the kind of people who are too sick to leave.

For this whole sector of my workload I had only one decision to make: whom to call. I was, of course, supposed to examine them before this but in practice it was much more convenient to let someone else make the diagnosis and then copy this onto the casualty card. It saved my time and the patient's and served my greater purpose of keeping the paperwork tidy.

This serious business out of the way I found I was free to deal with the small fry—the toddlers with beads up their noses, the children with lumps on their heads, the drunks, the overdoses, the cuts and sprains. The actual expertise you need for this kind of stuff could be written on the back of a cornflakes packet. For anything out of the ordinary I had time now to refer to the textbooks and could fall back in the end on Christine's good-natured prompting. She was always there when I needed her—teasing, laughing, never surprised by my ignorance. She turned out to be one of the few people in the world who don't use their knowledge as a weapon. Everyone exaggerates the complexity of their particular subject. I don't just mean doctors. I mean lecturers, car mechanics, cooker salesmen, airline pilots, bookies, builders . . . They think they'll lose status if they ever show you how simple it is. It takes the best brains in the country six years to train a casualty officer. But in the course of two weeks Christine taught me everything I needed to know. Well, almost everything. There are always complications.

CHAPTER
13

14th Feb.

Dear J,
Happy Valentine's Day. I liked this card and I didn't
have anyone else to send it to. I thought the bear looked
a bit like you. What do you mean, "undercurrents of
despair"? Too bad. If you find them depressing don't
read them—you're the only person I can be feeble with.
I thought you believed that love was measured in hon-
esty.

However, if you want idle chat I can give you
chat, let's see, what have I done that's wildly exciting
. . . well . . . The crocuses are coming out . . . um . . .
They're starting a season of Molière at the Old Vic.

Last night was Tartuffe—*not bad at all. I went to an opening at the King Street Gallery—ceramic reliefs, all a bit too fussy. I drove up the Wye Valley with a bunch of architects I know. Had tea. That's about it. The rest of the time I've been working.*

After a disastrous start the new doc seems to be shaping up. In fact I rather liked working with him in the end. He listens to my advice. He lets me do the stitching and he asks for help with the odd diagnosis which has to be a first. You've no idea what a difference it makes to the level of job satisfaction. They all talk about the Health Team but I've never met a doctor who doesn't see himself as the boss. I'd love to know what his background is. He behaves very oddly sometimes and I never know if he's a naïf pretending to be sophisticated or a sophisticate pretending to be naïve. He stopped me in the corridor the other day, all in a flap about being invited to the consultant's house for dinner tonight. Asking all sorts of strange questions about what to wear, what to talk about, what sort of wine to take. I told him just to be himself and he gave a hollow laugh . . . curiouser and curiouser . . .

Sorry, I shouldn't be covering your valentine card with stuff about another man but I know how voyeuristic you are so I'm sure you won't mind. Running out of space here but there's just enough room for some kisses on the bottom.

XXX Chris

CHAPTER
14

CROSS THE BRIDGE AND TURN RIGHT and you are descending through Clifton to the commercial heart of Bristol. Turn left and you are on Bristol Downs—acres of trees and rolling parkland bordered on its western side by the Gorge. Along the other three sides of the park are the most expensive houses in town—huge mausoleums built on the revenue from Madeira wine, American tobacco and African slaves.

This is where Mountford lived, in a beautiful bowfronted mansion, set back from the road behind a high beech hedge. The lawn had reached the state of perfection that can only be accomplished by professional gardeners. His Bentley was parked on the honey-colored gravel of the front drive with his wife's Metro just in front of it. I lifted the brass lion's-head knocker and let it

fall—half expecting a butler to answer the door—but
Mountford answered it himself, grinning and laughing in
a gray mohair cardigan with a silk cravat. I'd worn my
suit and immediately felt overdressed.

He took me through to the lounge, which was car-
peted from the Adam fireplace to the bay window in
acres of dark blue Axminster. His wife got up and met
me halfway from the door. Mountford was already moving the drinks trolley.

"Celia—this is Simon."

She took my hands between hers. She was a broad
woman but both her bearing and her clothes were suffi-
ciently elegant to disguise the fact. A pile of gray hair was
held on top of her head apparently by a single pin. She
looked about ten years younger than Mountford and
must once have been quite a looker. She had an un-
affected smile and delicate crow's feet around her eyes.

"I always insist that Benny introduce me to all his
new young doctors. We don't have any children of our
own."

Benny. I'd wondered in the past what the B stood
for. It wasn't the name I'd expected but, on reflection, it
was strangely appropriate.

"Come and sit by the fire," she said, taking my arm—
one of these harmless flirtatious gestures that women of a
certain age enjoy with younger men. Mountford seemed
touchingly besotted with her and was always fussing
about, refilling her drink or passing her the olives.

"So how are you finding the work?"

"I was a bit shaky at first but now I'm getting into the
swing of it."

"I'm sure you're just being modest. Benny says
you're very efficient."

I shrugged in a self-deprecating manner, sipped my
gin and looked around the room for ammunition. I'd
been cornered by Hillary in the doctors' bar the day before and was learning fast that the only way to avoid awk-

ward questions was to keep lobbing balls in the opposite
direction. With the Mountfords it looked as though this
was going to be easy. The room contained, neatly arranged, all the trophies of their rich and varied lives—an
African mask, a photo of a dinner party on some Medi-
terranean patio, a stuffed fox with an engraved silver inscription on the base, a huge oil painting of a stretch of
Scottish moorland, a wedding invitation, a number of
framed portraits . . . there was enough material here to
keep me going all evening.

"It's a lovely place you've got," I began.

"Yes, we like it," Celia said. "Where do you come
from yourself?"

"Oh, London. Just south of London."

"Did you go to school there?"

"Yes."

"Which school?"

"Filbourne."

"Filbourne!" Celia Mountford clapped her hands as
if an ace had been served. She'd had a lot more practice
at this kind of game than I'd ever had and I should have
realized then that I was out of my league. But the fire was
roaring, the gin was warming and a blustery wind was
hurling rain against the window. I settled into the arm-
chair and asked, "You know Filbourne?"

"Oh, yes, we've been there, haven't we, Benny?" with
which Celia Mountford launched into a catalog of friends
whose children and grandchildren had been there.

For five or ten minutes we played "Did you know so-
and-so?" and "Surely so-and-so would have been in your
year." I stumbled through this, claiming passing acquain-
tance with two of the names she threw up and wondering
how I could possibly abort the conversation. All my attempts at diversion failed. The Mountfords belonged to
the same social stratum as Simon's parents and enjoyed
nothing more than unpicking these intricate links: school,
profession, money and history meshed together in a net-

work of Masonic complexity and, as we followed one strand, then another, I saw that it constituted a more frightening test of authenticity than anything the medical profession might have exposed me to. If anything, the discussion about home was worse than the discussion about school.

"Where did you say you lived?"

"Headley Down," I said.

"Which side?" asked Celia.

I mouthed silently.

"Well, you must know the Flockharts, they live in the big Lutyens house just off the A twenty-three."

"I know the house but I've never met your friends."

"Don't your parents hunt?"

"No," I said, hoping against hope that Simon's parents didn't. Holy God, what if they did know Celia Mountford's friends?

"Well, tell me where their house was—I'm sure Isla would know it."

I finished my second gin with a gulp. "Sorry," I said. "Can I use your bathroom?"

I hid upstairs, playing for time. While I was there I had a snoop in their bedroom. They still slept in a double bed. Mountford wore dark-green silk pajamas and Celia had a big white lacy thing. There was a print of naked peasant girls above their bed. I heard Celia Mountford leave the lounge and go into the kitchen. I took a deep breath, adjusted my tie, and went back down.

"Nettle soup. I fell in love with her because of her nettle soup." This was Mountford speaking. We were sitting in their dining room with a big log fire in the grate. The rain continued to applaud against the window. There were pictures of Mountford's Bristolian ancestors on the duck-egg walls. The family had been in banking for generations, which explained the money. Mountford's great-grandfather was the one who'd really struck it rich by investing in the Great Western Railway—he was the one with the muttonchop whiskers, seated above the fireplace, fingering his fob.

We sat around the oval table. I was facing great-grandfather. Celia was on my right and Mountford was on my left. The conversation about Mountford's lineage got us through the soup. Celia wouldn't accept any help with bringing in the next course so I stayed with Mountford. It was then that he got on to the subject of university.

"Ah, yes, Cambridge," he said, pushing back his seat and folding his hands on his neat potbelly. "I was at Balliol myself. Happy days, happy days. I daresay you took part in the bumps?"

"Oh yes. I did a lot of that."

"Where did you row?"

"On the canal," I said.

"You mean the river."

"Yes. Of course. The river."

"But which position?"

"It varied," I said.

"I was number three. I was thinner then, of course"—he giggled and patted his abdomen affectionately—"just the college eight. What college did you say you belonged to?"

"Clare," I said.

"That's right . . . yes . . . yes . . . now. I always forget. It's been years since I was there last. Which one is Clare?"

"You know," I said, sensing disaster, ". . . on the river . . ."

"Which side of King's?"

"On the left."

"You mean left looking from King's Street . . . going toward Trumpington, that is?"

"Yes," I said.

I'd been vague about Headley Down but I was totally

ignorant about Cambridge. In fact, my only points of reference were the photos in Simon's album—a grassy quadrangle, an ornate stone bridge. I had no idea where any of this stood in relation to anything else but had formed the notion that the town was a kind of ribbon development along the Cam. I looked up and saw Mountford's great-grandfather looking down his nose at me—an imperious, impatient-looking man, sitting above me like a judge with me in the position of the prisoner and Mountford as the prosecuting counsel.

"Describe it to me. . . . Is it the red-brick one just over the bridge from that pub . . . the Anchor—yes?"

"That's right," I retaliated. "Which college did *you* go to?"

"I went to Oxford, Balliol. I told you that."

The mistake threw me and I didn't get another question in. I was reminded how, in my original interview, Mountford's friendly bonhomie had in fact been more worrying than Thorn's inquisition. Now his smooth, bald forehead furrowed, dislodging his spectacles and he said, "No. No no no . . . that's not Clare, I'm sure it's not. The one I'm describing is Queens'." Then he called through to the kitchen, "Celia, describe Clare College, Cambridge, to me."

She came in carrying a casserole dish. "It's that stone one down the path behind the Senate House."

"No, no," said Mountford pleasantly, "Simon says it's brick."

"Well, he must be confusing it with somewhere else," she said pleasantly, taking off the lid and inhaling the steam.

Mountford passed a plate to me and took one himself. "Of course he's not. He went there."

Celia looked at me again. "Help yourself to vegetables," she said.

"You did," Mountford told me, "You said it was a red-brick one on the far side of the Cam."

"Thank you," I said to Celia, and then to Mountford, "I'm terribly sorry. I must have misled you."

"But you said it was over the river," Mountford sounded belligerent.

"We were approaching it from opposite sides."

"No, we weren't. I'm sorry. We weren't."

Celia gave him new potatoes and string beans without asking if he wanted them, then offered me gravy as she helped herself.

Mountford got up and left the table.

"It's entirely my fault," I said, once he had left. "I don't know what I was thinking of."

"It's a bit warm in here, isn't it?" She got up and turned down the fire by means of a gas tap at the side of the fireplace. I'd been sure until then that it was real. Now I leaned across to examine it more closely. I wondered what Mountford was doing.

Celia caught my eye and put a hand on my arm. "I'm sorry," she said. "He gets things mixed up. You probably heard."

"No," I said.

She ate a piece of chicken thoughtfully.

The grandfather clock in the hallway chimed the half hour and another volley of rain rattled the window. Celia sipped her wine. "Well, you're bound to hear this," she said, "so I might as well explain it. . . . Until two years ago Benny was very involved with the Accident Department. He used to potter about there all day seeing patients—it was what he liked—being a sort of GP. He had his little consulting room and he'd check the ones who went back for regular treatment. Then he made a few mistakes—not bad mistakes but . . . you know. As you can see, he sometimes gets in a muddle. Some of the more militant young doctors complained about him and said he should be retired. So this was suggested by the Management Committee . . ."

The door that led through to the lounge creaked but

did not open fully. She rose from her seat, checked there was no one there, and gently closed the door, shutting out her husband and, in the same movement, entering a new level of intimacy with me.

"They offered to retire him on quite a generous pension but, of course, the money wasn't important to him. Benny felt insulted and got on his high horse and said that there were lots of other doctors older and less competent than he was. Which is true. So he refused to shift and the hospital was in a bind because obviously it would be embarrassing to all concerned if they sacked him and the junior doctors wouldn't . . . Have you heard all this before? . . . No, they wouldn't back down.

"So what happened was that Charles Thorn, who's really got his work cut out with intensive care, agreed to oversee the department . . . vetoing staff . . . checking treatment records. . . . This was sold to Benny as being a way of freeing him to work with patients, but Charles monitors everything. Benny's still allowed to do his clinic but he knows he no longer has any responsibility . . ."

We heard Mountford entering the lounge from another part of the house—probably his study. With a hostess's perfect timing Celia finished her sentence in the time it took Mountford to reach the dining room: ". . . except for small things—maintenance of equipment and so on. . . . Would you like some more?"

"No, thanks," I said as Mountford entered. "That was delicious."

Mountford came in carrying a heavy leather-bound volume which he rested on the table and squinted at over his glasses.

"'Clare,'" he read. "'Cambridge college founded in . . .' Where is it? . . . ah . . . 'situated between King's and Trinity . . . built of stone . . . backs on to the Cam.'"

"Yes," said Celia brightly. "I'm sure that's what Simon said."

"No, it's not," said Mountford.

"Eat your chicken before it gets cold," Celia told him.

"You said . . ." Mountford began, waving his fork at me.

Celia Mountford turned her bright, tapered eyes on him and said, very deliberately, "Simon was just telling me about his holidays."

"Yes, I've just spent a couple of weeks in Scotland," I said, taking my cue without faltering.

"Benny worked in Edinburgh when he was taking his membership, didn't you, darling?"

Mountford continued to frown for a second or two, then shrugged and closed the book.

We retired to the lounge with the lamps turned low and the firelight flickering on the cornices. The leather armchairs were pushed around the fire. Mountford sat with his legs apart, his wife with her legs tucked up underneath her and her woolen skirt arranged over her knees.

Mountford got on to the subject of local history and told me about the Llandugger Trow on Bristol Docks where Stevenson set the departure scene in *Treasure Island* and about the catacombs under the city where the slaves were kept in chains ready to be exported and about the *SS Great Britain* and Wookey Hole. Celia talked about her garden and about the small shooting estate they owned in Perthshire. In return I spun some yarns about Scotland, based largely on anecdotes of Alec's. For the purpose of these stories I converted his family's tenement into a substantial country house and gave Alec a junior partnership in a Glasgow law firm called Howell and Harris—my parents' surnames.

I ended the evening standing in front of their huge fireplace with a Havana cigar and a malt whiskey. Outside the rainstorm had passed and I imagine when I said good-bye, refused their offers to drive me back and walked off down the semicircular drive, that Celia

Mountford would tell her husband what a pleasant young man I was and how they must have me again.

I was equally sure they'd never have entertained a theater orderly like that.

A couple of days later I went down to the library on College Green.

I was walking back up Jacob's Wells Road toward the Triangle when I met Christine. I didn't recognize her out of her nurse's uniform and was initially horrified to see a stranger waving at me from outside the junk shop on the other side of the road. I was contemplating running for it when she took off her hat and I saw who it was.

"Hello, what are you doing?" she asked.

"Oh, just getting some books."

"Can I see?"

I showed her.

"How was your dinner with the Mountfords?" she asked.

"Interesting."

"Did she cook nettle soup?"

"Yes."

"I've heard she does nettle soup," said Christine.

"She's quite a lady," I said. "Not what I expected."

She smiled. "You mean sexier than Mountford?"

Her very use of the word seemed to acknowledge for the first time the possibility between us.

I laughed. "It's hard to be less sexy than Mountford."

"What's the house like?"

"Haven't you been there?"

"Where—the Mountfords? No. Celia doesn't trust me."

"Why not?"

"She thinks I'm one of the people who complained about her husband."

"And were you?" I asked.

"God, no," she said. "I'd only just started working in Bristol then. Anyway, I thought it was rather shabby the

way they held him responsible for the mistakes. If anything went wrong during my shift I'd regard it as my own
responsibility."

"That's very noble of you," I said.

"I'm not noble," she said. "I'm vain. I'm stubborn."

"Who says?"

She didn't answer.

CHAPTER
15

1st March

Dear J

They've reopened the Spa complex in the center of Bath. I love it there, you can have cream teas in the Pump Room and listen to a string quartet and read by the pools—wonderful steaming turquoise water, colonnades and Roman statues—well, it's all phony Victoriana of course but the effect's the important thing, isn't it? I wish you were here to share it with. Maybe I'll take Simon Hennessey.

I don't know what it is about that guy. You must think I fancy him the way I write about him all the time. I think I feel rather proprietorial about him. He doesn't seem to have many friends and I don't think he

87

goes out much. He told me he spends a lot of time studying but I don't know for what. I met him the other day coming back from the library with two books, one on Cambridge and one on English public schools. Funny, he's normally very loath to talk about his past and he doesn't seem like the kind of guy who'd wallow in nostalgia.

The air is lovely and fresh and the hospital grounds are full of daffodils. This is the time of year when all the geriatrics have a go at walking outside, then they fall down and break their hips, the poor old sticks. There are pigeons smooching all over the place. I can hear them in the department. We're on morning shift so there's a bit of time to get out and get fit. I should get a bicycle but there are so many hills here it would be like cycling in Highgate.

I'll be up as usual the weekend after next. If I don't hear from you I'll just arrive on Friday night and we can spend Saturday and Sunday together. Yum yum. Can't wait.

See you then, cookie.

Lots of love,
Christine

CHAPTER
16

At work my first great breakthrough had been learning to delegate; my second was cracking the code. In order to read McLeod's *Clinical Examination* I got Black's *Medical Dictionary* out of the hospital library. In it I discovered a section on medical abbreviations and gradually the casualty cards which the other doctors wrote began to make sense: I copied out some of Hillary's and began, word by word, to piece it all together:

C/o: *(This patient complains of)* 3/7 *(three days')* dysuria *(pain on passing urine)*. S/E *(systemic inquiry reveals that)* P.U. *(he/she passes urine)* x6/day *(six times a day)*. O bld *(There is no blood)*.

O/E *(On examination)* C/V, Resp. NAD *(no abnormality was detected in the heart or lungs)*. Abdo OKOK *(On abdominal examination neither kidney was palpable)*. IX MSU

(Investigation consisted of a midstream urine specimen). Δ
U.T.I. *(Diagnosis: urinary tract infection).* Rx *(Treatment:)*
Septrin ii b.d. *(Two tablets of Septrin twice a day).*

You see doctors scrawling out this kind of thing and
it looks impenetrably complex. In fact, it's extremely simple, and the reason they abbreviate it out of recognition is
because they write more or less the same thing every time
they see a woman with cystitis.

Here's a man with back pain:

> C/o 3/7 Low back pain, (lifting cement)
> S/E P.U. normal, o. anes. o Sciatica.
> O/E C/v. Resp. NAD
>   G.I. OLOKOKOS. Nil palp. o tender. PR NAD.
>   o saddle anes.
>   Loco. o deformity. tender L4/5. SLR L=R=90
>   Neuro. Power, tone. reflexes. sensation, NAD
> XR NAD.
> Δ   Back strain
> Rx   Bed rest.

Once you can read this it tells you everything you need to
know about examination and treatment. Having sussed
this out, the letters that some patients brought from their
GPs became a new mine of information. Sometimes I was
able to copy them directly onto the casualty cards. If the
patient seemed seriously ill I'd call the specialist. If not
I'd send them home. That's all general medicine consists
of—a bit of reassurance and a bit of guesswork. The rest
is magical symbols.

I was never summoned back to Thorn's office. In
fact, I hardly saw him after that first encounter. I avoided
him in the dining room and, as long as things went
smoothly, he rarely visited the department. I can only
assume my casualty cards had convinced him I was

doing my job. I moved on to mornings, then afternoons, then nights again, changing over with Hillary and the sleek young man called Adam. I avoided the other doctors and spent all my spare time reading around the cases I'd seen. Every day I added to my repertoire of skills. I could rattle off the systemic inquiry. I could mime my way through a brief physical examination and I was getting some basic ideas about prescribing. Hitherto I'd been daunted by the sheer number of drugs available but it soon became apparent that you could get by with about a dozen. I learned the dosage for three or four antibiotics, a couple of painkillers, a sleeping pill, an aerosol for asthma, a skin cream, and two treatments for indigestion. That covered 90 percent of patients. Of course it was all pretty hit and miss. I wasn't really practicing medicine—all I had mastered was the pretense of practicing medicine. It wasn't till Mr. Gough that I realized the difference.

It was the beginning of March and my shift coincided with Christine's again. I knew from my dinner with the Mountfords how easy it was to give too much away and her ability to engage in conversation was beginning to make me nervous. I was almost relieved when I turned up the first afternoon and found, in place of Christine, a young student nurse called Miriam. By this time I could just about keep my head above water even without assistance. I moved from cubicle to cubicle treating the injuries I was familiar with and busking through the ones I wasn't.

The noise of the ambulance didn't bother me at first—I assumed it was heading for the entrance—direct referral to one of the wards. I watched it slow down at the far side of the bridge, then race across the sky toward me. They raised the barrier nearest me and I lost sight of it, expecting the noise to fade as the ambulance turned round the back of the hospital. But this time it didn't fade. I heard it grow louder and louder till the blue light filled the doctors' room. Then the doors were crashing open and two ambulance men were coming up the corridor, bulky men in black nylon jackets dwarfing the old man on the stretcher between them.

One of them called to me as they bowled past into resus. I hurried after them, forgetting my stethoscope. I turned and went back for it. As I bent to pick it up some pens spilled out of my pocket on to the office floor. I left them there and drove myself along the corridor.

"Mr. Gough," said one of the ambulance men as I pushed through the swing doors. "Aged sixty-five. Suddenly became breathless in bed tonight. His wife phoned us up."

He finished jacking up the ambulance trolley and they lugged him across onto the black plastic cushions of the resus table. Mr. Gough had looked tiny on the stretcher and now, with the blankets off, he looked smaller still—a ribbed, white scrap of a man, his eyes rolling, his chest heaving. When he coughed tenacious pink froth came out of his mouth and trickled down the concavity of one cheek. His wiry arms clawed the air as if trying to ward off some shadowy assassin. One ambulance man retrieved the stretcher pole as the other locked up the sides of the trolley. I realized they were leaving me alone with him.

"Wait!" I said.

"Yes?"

"No—sorry, nothing," I said weakly and they left, their heavy footsteps fading down the corridor toward the door.

Meanwhile Gough was dying before my eyes. I didn't have the first idea what I should do. When I reached for his pulse he turned his wild, unfocused eyes on me and made a grab for my sleeve. I fought him off and he fell back coughing. Now he was shaking in some kind of fit. His old chest heaved like an ancient concertina pulling against clogged valves.

"Is there anything I should do?" said a small voice. I'd forgotten about Miriam. She was standing at the farthest end of the room with her hands folded and her eyes as big as soup plates.

"Ring the medics."

"I've already rung them."

I knew from past experience that they could take fifteen minutes to arrive. The only way of getting them there more quickly was by paging the cardiac-arrest team but the old bugger wasn't dead enough for that.

"Well, take his blood pressure," I said.

Miriam set about this, looking relieved to have some function and I wished I'd taken his blood pressure myself. At least it would have given me something to do. I didn't care if Gough died. In fact I dearly wanted him to die. But I didn't want to be looking idle when it happened.

I noticed the oxygen cylinder. He was breathless. I could give him oxygen.

I turned on the tap under the trolley, untangled the green plastic tubing and strapped the hissing mask over his face. His hand caught it and dragged it off. I pushed it back on and he began scrabbling at my fingers. It was impossible. No progress had been made. I pictured the medics arriving, Gough still dying, me hanging around uselessly with my hands in my pockets. I remembered Simon saying that death is acceptable as long as somebody can be seen to be doing something. He was right.

A drip. I could try and put up a drip!

"Run through a bag of dextrose," I said to Miriam. A smile lit up her face. She obviously knew that routine. I wished I shared her confidence. I'd held countless arms when drips were being put up but I'd never actually done it myself. The process had always fascinated me—threading a slim plastic tube over a needle and into an arm vein. It had always seemed very easy, but since my abortive attempts at stitching I'd learned to mistrust such impressions.

I started rummaging about in the drawers looking for a Venflon intravenous catheter. I found needles, blood tubes, airways—no Venflons. I became frantic, dragging the drawers out and rifling through them like a burglar who hears footsteps on the stairs. I could hear Miriam priming the plastic drip tube with dextrose solution and Gough, behind me, choking on more froth.

I finally found the Venflons in a drawer above the sink. The drawer fell out and I left it there—the rest of its contents strewn over the wet linoleum. The needle was three inches long and looked, in my panic, to be a centimeter thick.

Lying high on the stretcher Gough wrestled blindly with death. Miriam was taking the blood pressure again.

"Eighty over fifty," she said.

The figures meant nothing to me. I grabbed the other arm and wrapped a tourniquet around it. The veins jumped out at me. I held the needle close and stabbed at one—nothing. I stabbed at the vein again and, miraculously, the needle went in. I threaded the plastic catheter over it and Gough's blood starting spurting over my hand.

"Give me the thing . . . the whatnot . . . the tube!"

"The drip set," said a female voice.

I looked round and saw Christine standing very close with the drip in one hand. She twisted it on to the end of my catheter, switched on the flow of dextrose and took off the tourniquet.

"It looks as though a typhoon's hit this place," she said. "Here, I'll tape that on. Help me sit him up."

We lifted the back of the trolley and she raised the sides to stop Gough from falling out.

"I couldn't find where anything was kept," I said.

"Obviously. Keep him upright. What do you want now? Frusemide? Morphine?"

Without waiting for my answer she was unlocking the drugs cupboard. I grunted noncommitally and pretended to be doing something with my stethoscope. Listening to Gough's chest I could hear the noise like crumpling tissue paper.

Christine came back with a syringe full of oily yellow fluid. "Eighty milligrams," she said.

Eighty milligrams of what? And where did it go? In the drip? In a vein? In a muscle? Miriam was watching me like a small startled bird. I knew from the books that some drugs were lethal intravenously and I had no way of knowing if this was one of them. I didn't even know what it was. On the other hand, Gough obviously needed something fast.

I looked across to Christine, hoping she would offer some clue but she had turned her back on me to write something in the ledger. I told Miriam to clear the spilled syringes off the floor and went for a vein. If I killed Gough I could always say the drug hadn't worked. I took hold of his wrist and squirted the liquid into the rubber bung before anyone could see me.

Gough didn't seem to get any worse but neither was he any better, his eyes were straining from their sockets and his pupils were like pinpricks.

Christine came back, squinting at the gradations on two syringes. "Morphine five and Stemetil twelve point five," she said, handing them to me.

I put them into Gough's wrist as well. It was the quickest way of getting rid of the stuff.

Christine wasn't looking. She was stroking Gough's horrible sweat-smeared forehead and saying, "There, there, we'll have you all right soon," as if it were remotely possible that the old bugger would haul himself back from the grave.

I didn't know what to do next so I looked around for somewhere to dispose of the needles.

"Just leave that," she said. "I'll put the ECG leads on if you call X-ray."

I left, glad to be out of the charnel house.

At my sister's wedding, one of my mother's friends asked me to dance. The band was playing "Fly Me to the Moon." I tried to refuse but she insisted so we clattered on to the dance floor. We did an almost perfect foxtrot followed by a waltz and she commented how nice it was to find someone of my generation who knew the old steps. In fact I'd never done a foxtrot in my life before but she was so good at it that neither she, nor anyone watching, had realized. There is something infectious about absolute competence—the information is transferred without either party being aware of the exchange. Working with Christine was that kind of experience.

I phoned the X-ray girl and she said she'd be right round, then I bleeped the medical SHO again.

A posh Indian voice answered the phone.

"Hello, it's Simon Hennessey in Casualty."

"Yes, sorry, I'm rather tied up here, what have you got?"

"An old boy, he's a bit breathless." I was rarely asked to be more specific. It is fashionable among doctors to use this kind of nonmedical understatement between themselves. "I've given him morphine and Frusemide and . . ." another hiatus while I tried to remember the third drug but its name escaped me ". . . and he doesn't seem to be getting any better . . ." I said.

"What's the ECG show?"

"The nurse is just doing it."

"OK," he said, "I'll be right along." Then he put the phone down.

I hung around in the doctors' room for a while longer, reluctant to tempt fate any further with my charade of treating Mr. Gough. I gave him a couple more minutes to die properly before going back in.

Christine handed me a roll of pink paper. "Inferior MI," she said and turned to detach the monitor leads. I took it from her but didn't look at it. Instead I was looking past her to where Gough was sitting, pink now, gulping air like a marathon runner, sweat pouring from him but alive and breathing nevertheless. I walked over to him, slipping on some of the pink froth he'd spewed up. I pushed the drip stand out of the way to get close to him. I couldn't believe the transformation.

Christine clipped the top back on the ECG machine and turned to Mr. Gough. "This is Dr. Hennessey, the doctor who saved your life."

Gough seemed to register this because he pawed gratefully at my sleeve and made some shapes with his lips. I felt my eyes fill with foolish tears. As an orderly I'd seen a couple of births and their effect was much the same. Come to think of it, the event was almost the same. Gough had looked no more like a human being when they wheeled him in through those doors than one of the floppy, bloody newborns. And seeing him now taking his first breaths was like hearing that first eye-pricking cry.

I pressed my eyes with the balls of my thumbs and patted him on the shoulder, then blundered back out through the swing doors to make myself some coffee. While I was pouring it the Indian doctor came down the corridor. He introduced himself as Kassim.

"What have we got here then?"

"Inferior MI, I've fixed him up now."

"Good-oh," he said and took the ECG strip from me. I wrote out the casualty card while I could still remember most of the long words.

The phrase Christine had used was 'pulmonary edema'. Once Gough had been taken to the wards and Christine was clearing up I looked it up in the dictionary. This is what it said:

> PULMONARY EDEMA: *An accumulation of fluid in the lungs (see above for causes). The symptoms include increasing breathlessness which is relieved by sitting upright. The classic signs are pink frothy sputum, raised neck veins and basal crepitations. Treatment is with oxygen, Frusemide and morphine.*

Reading this I was reminded of the lines from the systemic inquiry:

"Do you feel breathless?"
"What makes it better?"
"What makes it worse?"

I remembered standing with Alec outside some curtains at the West Harwood Hospital.

"Do you feel breathless?"
"Yes."
"What makes it better?"
"Sitting up."
"What makes it worse?"
"When I lie flat."
"Do you bring up any spit?"
"Yes."
"What color is it?"
"Pink."

Fluid in the lung is called pulmonary edema. The listed causes included heart failure and liver failure. The man at the West Harwood had heart failure. I'd seen liver failure too—I remember quaking under Thorn's interrogation on the subject of Mr. Weatherilt.

"What can you hear?"

"Basal crepitations."

I'd known it all along—I'd seen two cases. I knew what to listen for, I knew the questions to ask, and the treatment was written in the book. In an instant I was aware of the miraculous logic of it all—the systemic inquiry, the physical examination, the obscure foreign-sounding words—suddenly they all converged. If you made the right connections you could save a man's life. Even for a condition as fearsome as Gough's it was possible to follow a recipe. The scales had fallen from my eyes. I felt suddenly inspired. Like the magician's apprentice.

Christine came back, drying her hands on her skirt.

"Are you all right?" she asked.

"Fine, fine."

She crossed the room and closed the window. Outside the sun was setting. She stood for a while with her eyes closed letting the sun play on her face.

I said, "You're an unusual person to be a nurse."

"You speak as though you've known a lot of nurses."

"Just professionally," I said.

"In what way unusual?" she asked, turning from the window.

I said, "More eccentric," and she raised one eyebrow.

"It's not a career that fosters individuals," I explained. "They don't usually like people who do things their own way."

"They don't like me," she said. "That's why they put me in the Accident Department."

"I would have thought it was impossible to dislike you."

"Why do you say that?" she asked.

"You seem so . . . angelic."

She laughed. "That's not what the nuns said."

"What nuns?"

"At school."

"You went to a convent?"

"I had a rather unorthodox education, a convent followed by drama school. What about you?"

"Grammar . . . I mean a public school."

"Where about?"

"Filbourne, it's called Filbourne. Where was yours?"

"Manchester. Our Lady of the Sacred Heart."

"Where did you study acting?"

"London."

"Do you ever go back there?"

"Every three weeks."

"Is that where your parents live?"

"No, I go to see my Uncle Jack. He lives all alone and
doesn't have a phone. So I write him letters and visit
him."

"That's very kind of you."

"It's not an effort. I love him to bits."

"How long were you an actress for?"

"Long enough," she said. "You don't want to know
about that—tell me about yourself."

I took a deep breath and launched into a fiction constructed from what I imagined of Simon's life and remembered of my own. It was peculiarly exhilarating to be
completely in control of my own history. I transposed a
couple of my own school experiences onto the set of Filbourne School, my own few happy memories of Manchester University onto my mental picture of Cambridge,
and what evolved was as novel to me as it was to Christine.

We talked, on and off, until the shift ended at ten. I
can picture her sitting in the corner of the doctors' room

so she could be near the intercom and see down the corridor to the main entrance. My chair was by the window. We were probably only a few feet apart but it felt like miles. I remember constantly changing position, smiling till my cheeks ached, Christine in her tight blue uniform and black stockings, her slender legs crossed so that the calf of one fell almost parallel with the shin of the other. She had a habit of pinching the skin of one arm which I found inexplicably erotic. The memory of my evening with the Mountfords was still fresh in my mind and I knew that every lie I embarked on was a hostage to fortune but I found I couldn't stop myself. Our success with old Gough had intoxicated me beyond caution.

CHAPTER
17

22nd March

Dear J,
I never thought I'd allow myself to get jaded but I obviously have. We had an old guy through the department close to death with breathing problems and we fixed him up and sent him off to the wards and I must have just thought, "Oh well that's another one out of the way—what's next?" Because I came back to the doctors' room and was amazed to find Simon Hennessey, the new doc, looking all emotional and grinning from ear to ear. How do you hold on to that—the ability to still be inspired? You do it—I think men are naturally less cynical than women. When I saw him I remembered how I used to feel after a really fantastic

performance when everything comes together and the play takes off. I miss that and I know that I used to get it from this job. What a terrible thing when you can't even get excited by saving someone's life.

Anyway we sat down, Simon Hennessey and I, and we had a long chat. Normally he's very reluctant to open out but this time he was really buzzing. There's still something odd about him—I've always felt he's holding something back, as though there's some awful dark secret he's afraid might spill out.

Maybe it's just my overactive imagination. Or maybe you're right—that he just fancies me and I make him nervous because of that. Anyway I told him I really admired his attitude to the work and thought that he was twice as inspired and open-minded as most of the other doctors in this place and he told me what a great help I'd been to him so I've got a new friend now and we're going down to Wells this weekend which is beautiful in the spring.

I've not heard from you for a bit so I'm assuming the 29th is OK. Write or call me if there are any problems. You know you're still really the only man in my life.

Love and kisses,
Christine

CHAPTER 18

MARCH DISSOLVED INTO APRIL. EVERY DAY it had been getting slightly warmer—limpid spring sunlight massaging the frosted earth back to life. Suddenly you could buy daffodils on Princess Victoria Street. I had the feeling myself of coming out of the shade. My old recurring nightmare of meeting someone who knew me from London had faded like a memory of winter. I had spent my first two pay checks on a secondhand Triumph Herald Convertible and asked Christine to come for a drive.

I'd never been to her house before and it took me some time to find the address. I eventually located it at the far end of a short, blind crescent which curved, like an appendix, off Royal Terrace. On one side there was a high privet hedge with communal gardens beyond. On the other stood a row of wedge-shaped townhouses with tall windows on three stories and glazed semicircular porchways on the ground floor.

The house she lived in was different from the rest. Its porchway was square and supported by four pillars. A paved walkway led round the far end of the building beyond which trees and undergrowth went tumbling into the Gorge. I pushed on the heavy wooden door and it opened. There were no bells for the various flats and I couldn't find the light for the hallway. I waited for a second till my eyes grew accustomed to the twilight, then closed the door behind me. The stair curved upward, giving out at its widest part on to a small locked conservatory with a tattered banana tree inside. On one of the panes of glass was a small green etching of a mermaid. I continued upward in the dappled half-light. The ceiling high above my head was latticed with crumbling plaster moldings. There was a door at the top of the stairs with Christine's name on it. I rang the bell.

"Come in. Sorry. I'm not ready."

She was wearing a baggy woolen sweater and a pair of jeans. She said, "Go through. I'll just put some shoes on," then disappeared into a candy-striped bedroom. I walked into the lounge.

The room was the length of a cricket pitch and three times the width of one. The polished wooden floor was covered in rugs. As you walked in there was a Chinese screen on the left and a large oval dining table with round-backed Queen Anne chairs. An elaborate gilt mirror hung on the wall above the fireplace.

"It's not mine, it's all rented."

I turned and she was standing at the far end of the room in one of those strange, gauche postures she used to adopt, all her weight on one hip and her toes pointed in.

"How long have you lived here?" I had to raise my voice for it to carry the length of the room.

"Since I arrived. Two years. Do you want a cup of tea before we go?"

"Thank you."

I continued my tour of inspection while she was in the kitchen. The windows all faced south, overlooking the old docks. The shelves below were full of plays. There was a black-and-white cat on top of her bookshelves, which I'd thought, from a distance, to be a statue, but when I put a hand out to touch it, it bounded past me and took up residence on the mantelpiece.

There was a writing desk in front of the window. On top of it was a framed photograph with a rosary hooked over one corner.

"Tea?"

"Thank you."

She brought it across and noticed the photo I'd been looking at—herself in the center of a group of people, laughing, in a row boat. A man with a touch of gray in his beard had his arm around her shoulder.

"Where's that?" I asked.

"London, the Serpentine."

I didn't ask her *who* and she didn't volunteer the information. I rearranged the photo on top of the bookcase between the lacquer sewing box and the vase of dried flowers. It all seemed to belong. To be settled, assured. Christine arranged herself on the sofa. The cat came and sat on her lap and I thought of the places I'd lived in till then—mostly bare and undecorated and littered with clothes, usually a suitcase ill-concealed below the bed. That was my life too—stationary but unsettled, always at odds with my surroundings. Christine seemed perfectly at ease with hers.

I said, "Tell me why you gave up acting."

She was stroking the cat with one hand and it was wriggling and arching its back each time her hand passed over it.

"I wanted to be useful—to do something that would help."

"Catholic guilt?" I asked.

She shrugged and smiled.

A carpet of mist had lifted off the black fields and now hung uncertainly between the copses. In patches you could still see steam rising from the plowed earth. We had the roof down and our coat collars turned up. The cold slipstream cut in behind us, tugging at strands of Christine's hair and throwing them forward across her face. When I looked across she was laughing and smudges of red had appeared in each cheek.

"How are you getting on with Thorn?" she shouted.

"I don't know," I said. "He hardly ever speaks to me. I see him in the corridors and he might give a nod."

"He's like that with everyone. He's not very demonstrative."

"He is when he wants to be," I said. "What does he do in his spare time?"

"I don't think he has much spare time. He works an awful lot. I think he's got a place in Cornwall where he goes with his family."

"What's his wife like?"

"Nice. She's an invalid . . . she has multiple sclerosis . . . Thorn looks after her."

I was on the point of saying that that probably explained why he was so embittered but I checked myself, sensing that she admired and approved of Thorn. Personally I've never seen the point of devoting yourself to a basket case.

"And how are you getting on with Molly?" she asked.

"Oh, better."

"She's a good old stick," said Christine.

I nodded but didn't agree with that either. My own impression of Molly was that she was an interfering old bag. I still let her come into my room with tea and chatted with her when she wouldn't go away but secretly she filled me with revulsion. The other doctors went completely over the top, treating her as a sort of honorary aunt, sending her postcards when they went on leave and bringing her presents when they returned. I found the whole pantomime rather nauseating but realized that it would be unwise to alienate her.

"Yes," I said. "Good Old Molly."

It was spring. I could afford to be generous.

Wells is a cathedral town of cobbled streets and half-timbered houses. In its center is a park that contains the Bishop's Palace surrounded by a red stone wall and a moat. Beside this is the cathedral—you walk through an archway from the old town square and are confronted by the west front—a cliff face of statues and gargoyles in ornate masonry. They tell you not to put your faith in appearances, then they build something like that.

We walked round the nave, stopped under the spire and looked up at the tons of stone, suspended magically above us. There were huge iron wood-burning stoves in the aisles and I made Christine laugh by asking her if that was where they put the sinners.

Some conversations seem to hang suspended for minutes, hours, to be picked up again by common consent in the appropriate setting. In the cloisters of Wells Cathedral Christine said, without prompting, ". . . anyway it wasn't Catholic guilt, or not entirely; it was more a reaction to my friends. At drama school they were falling over themselves to be famous. Suddenly I couldn't see the point."

"Why did you want to be an actress in the first place?"

"There's a really good theater in Manchester. The Royal Exchange on Market Street."

"I know. I used to go there a lot."

"How come?"

"I spent a year in . . ." I bit my tongue but the sentence was already too obvious to abort.

"I spent a year in Manchester," I said.

"When was that?"

"Before university. I started studying biology, then changed to medicine at Cambridge."

She looked at me rather oddly. When I thought about it the story did seem pretty unlikely.

"You told me you went straight from school to Cambridge."

"I was unhappy in Manchester. I prefer to forget about it."

"So you're a year older than you said you were."

"No, I was a child prodigy."

She laughed at this and I quickly took the initiative.

"So tell me about drama school."

"Not much to tell," she said.

"You didn't enjoy it."

"Oh, I enjoyed it. I did then. While I believed in it. When we left, a few of us started an alternative theater group. Toured Holland. Got some grants from the Arts Council. We did some good stuff but they all secretly wanted to be TV personalities and appear on *Name That Tune.*"

"There's nothing wrong with wanting to be successful."

"You call that success, Simon?"

Every time she used my new name like that I remember feeling a rush of pleasure. "So you got disillusioned with acting?"

"Not with acting. With everything—the mood of the times. Sometimes I can't believe what's happened to our generation," she said. "Suddenly everyone's chasing rainbows. It doesn't matter if what they're doing is worth anything. They just want to be up there. You see something you like and you say, 'That should be me.' It's all image. People don't look inside themselves anymore."

"Look inside themselves for what?"

"For integrity, commitment, purpose—all those unfashionable things. Show me someone who still believes in decent anonymous toil for the common good."

I tried to think but the only person who came to mind was Alec.

"Thorn," she said. "It'll die out with his lot. That's what mass communication has done for us. We've devalued genuine work and replaced it with idle posturing."

"I'm not posturing," I said.

"I wasn't talking about you. I mean, is being a doctor still a high-status job?"

"Yes."

"No, it's not," she said, "and neither is nursing. You know what jobs have status these days—DJs, fashion models, chat-show hosts. The value of the work is nil but that's immaterial. People devote huge amounts of energy to completely useless endeavors—like those guys who jumped off the suspension bridge on elastic ropes or that kid who tried to shoot President Reagan—they'd rather do something dangerous or destructive, just to be noticed."

I said, "Maybe they just want to make an impression on the world."

"They'd have to be pretty desperate."

The subject was making me uneasy. I raked my mind for an alternative topic and remembered her photo of the man with the beard.

"Do you still see your acting friends?"

"Not really. They think I'm wasting my time and I think they're wasting theirs. Political drama—it's such a copout. Like all this stuff for Ethiopia. Pop concerts for Ethiopia. Fashion shows for Ethiopia. If people really cared they'd go there and help. No one even considers that. Same thing—the image of caring has replaced the need to care."

"Have you said that to them?"

"Of course I've said it. I used to say it all the time. Three years ago it was my party piece. After a while they said that if I felt so strongly I should do something about it—so here I am."

We had a cream tea in the square and drove home with the roof down and the sun setting over the Mendips. I dropped her off at her house and she got out, breathless and laughing, with her tangled hair all over her face.

"Thank you," she said. "It's been lovely."

"I'll see you then."

"Do you want to come up for a drink?"

"Yeah, OK."

She led me into the hallway. There was a table just inside the front door where mail was left and she picked up a letter addressed to her. When we got inside her flat I went to the loo and Christine went into the kitchen. When I came out she was looking pale and pinched and staring blankly at the envelope on the floor.

"Bad news?"

She looked up, startled, as though she'd forgotten I was there.

"Is there anything I can. . . ?"

She shook her head and crouched down to pick up the fallen envelope. She didn't look up again.

I touched her head. "Do you want me to go?"

She nodded.

"OK," I said. "I'll see you soon."

I let myself out.

CHAPTER
19

24th March

Dear J,
I can't believe this. Why didn't you tell me earlier? You know I would have come if only you'd asked. It's typical of you. You communicate so little. Like not having a phone and going on holiday alone. Why do you do that? And then this kind of thing out of the blue.

Anyway, I don't accept any of it. It's not the end, you're just being negative. I'll come up next weekend like I planned and we'll talk it through. I'd come sooner but I know they wouldn't let me off work. I can't bear the thought of losing you. I know we don't see much of each other but I depend on you. You're my only contact with the real world. All my love.

Christine

CHAPTER 20

I SAW CHRISTINE ON TWO OR three occasions the following week. She was working afternoons and I was working mornings so we'd cross over briefly at lunchtime. The letter, whatever it was, had transformed her. When I saw her the next day she had shadows under her eyes and the spring had gone out of her step. I asked her if she was OK and she smiled wanly. I would have liked to comfort her but I realized we weren't close enough. I patted her a couple of times, rather ineffectually—the kind of gesture that is meant to convey concern but is so devoid of intimacy that it only serves to remind both people of the distance between them. I rang her a couple of times but she wasn't answering the phone. I used to walk down the crescent she lived on and look up at the lights burning on the top floor but I never mustered the courage to ring her doorbell; instead I'd go for long walks through Clifton, all the way down to Hotwells Road and back up via the bars on Clifton Hill.

There was life on the streets now. The winter woolens had gone and the pubs were less crowded. I'd maybe sit on my own and read a book or put money in the jukebox, then walk back up to the hospital.

A couple of times that week I visited the bar in the doctors' residence but on both occasions the conversation drifted to school and university and the hospitals I'd supposedly worked at. Christine had never visited any of these places but even so she had spotted the odd inconsistency in my stories. Engaging in similar conversations in the doctors' mess would be nothing short of suicide. So I steered clear of the bar and kept to myself.

For the first time I began to feel lonely. Prior to that, the whole thing had been so frenetic and highly charged that I hadn't had time to think about a social life but now I missed company. One evening I got as far as picking up the phone to call Alec but I put it down again as soon as he answered. He'd never have believed I was speaking from the Caribbean. I told myself that I'd severed my connections with my past. If I wanted friends I had to reconstruct all that. I needed to do some field research.

I left Bristol on Friday afternoon and spent the night in a bed-and-breakfast in Winchester. I found Filbourne the next morning—a sleepy village on the edge of the New Forest. The landlord of the Fleece and Firkin directed me to Filbourne School—a Jacobean building in brick and stone. There were wisps of smoke still emerging from the tall bunches of chimneys. A group of small, self-confident boys were sitting on the low wall that bordered the front driveway. I introduced myself and one of them, called Fentiman, said he'd show me round.

I followed him down an avenue of pollarded trees to the main door. As we walked, Fentiman told me in a clear, high voice that there were eight hundred boys in the school, all of them boarders. He explained the coat of arms above the main door, pointed out the roll of honor painted on the wall of the main hall, described the cantilever principle behind the construction of the grand staircase, identified the part of the banister rail that had been damaged in a near-fatal accident, climbed on heating pipes to show me, above the blanked-out panes of glass, the interior of the locked classrooms and finally took me down to the dining room to introduce me to the kitchen staff.

It was here that my diminutive guide ran into one of the masters.

"Fentiman, what do you think you're doing?"

"I'm showing Mr. Harris round the school."

"And who, pray"—the cloaked man turned his small eyes on me—"is Mr. Harris?"

"Matthew Harris," I said. "I'm a friend of one of your old boys. I was passing by and . . . he's often talked about the school . . . I thought I'd visit."

"Which old boy? See me later," said the master, still looking at me as Fentiman scuttled away.

"Dr. Simon Hennessey," I said.

"Not one of mine," said the master. "We do have official visiting days at the school. At all other times these buildings are out of bounds to all but boys and the parents of boys."

"I'm sorry," I said. "I'll see myself out."

"Well . . . as you're here," said the master who was, in the final analysis, as eager as young Fentiman for a change from routine, "I may as well show you round."

I left three hours later, having visited the chapel, the rugby fields, the swimming pool, the gymnasium and, finally, the dining room for lunch.

I drove to Petersfield along the A272, then up the A3 as far as Hindhead, which turned out to have the nearest hotel to Headley Down. I spent most of the eve-

ning writing all I could about Filbourne School in a hard-
backed jotter.

Headley Down was simpler. I'd passed through it before and vaguely remembered the small village square,
the row of alms cottages and the church. I checked and
made a note of the name of the minister and the names
of the various shopkeepers. I looked in the road guide
for places of interest I might be expected to know and
found listed, among other minor country houses, the
place where Celia Mountford's friends lived. I drove past
it and peered in through the driveway just in case it ever
came up in conversation again.

I gave London a wide berth on my way up north and
it was past midnight when I arrived at the Blue Boar
Hotel.

Cambridge—that vision of cloistered bliss has become everyone's expectation of university and now, visiting the
place for the first time, I understood its potency. It was
the last week of term and the streets were thronged with
bicycles—ringing and rattling over the cobbles, stacked
against the college walls. I found Clare, as Mountford
had correctly described it, down a lane between King's
and the Senate House. The college secretary told me the
name of Simon's tutor and the cleaning lady let me look
in his old room—a dark paneled bedsitter with a china
sink and a wall cupboard and a view out over the leaded
roofs. I took a copy of the college prospectus which told
me all the names of the members of staff—I didn't imagine they'd changed that much in five years—then I took a
bus out along Hills Road to New Addenbrookes Hospital,
borrowed a white coat and went for a stroll round the
doctors' mess, the dining room and the transplant unit. I
returned in the late afternoon to a wooden seat overlooking the Backs from where I was able to watch the students cutting across the lawns in groups of two and three

and listen to the conversations that floated down the slow, green waters of the Cam.

Before I left I stopped for a whiskey in the Three Bells on Trumpington Street. There were two printed cards pinned on the side of the bar. One advertised moonlight punting on the river, the other horse riding at Saffron Walden. It was just after opening time and the only other person at the bar was a man in a polo-neck jersey who introduced himself as Geoffrey Walker. He told me he was doing a Ph.D. on a sixteenth-century Italian composer called Gesualdo. I told him I'd studied medicine at Clare College and managed to convince him that I knew some of his friends there. When he invited me back for dinner I declined and said I had to get back to Bristol.

I drove back out across the fens to the M11 leaving the towers and spires of Cambridge behind me. I know that if I'd visited the place a few months earlier I'd have been seized with an unbearable ache of regret for the past I never had. But now I owned the place and, during the long drive back to Bristol, the images merged to produce a memory of Camelot more perfect than anything that could have existed in reality.

CHAPTER
21

CHRISTINE HAD BEEN AWAY FOR THE weekend. The lights of her flat were off when I arrived back in Bristol that Sunday night and Monday turned out to be her day off. I felt obscurely piqued by this. The trip in search of my past had been partly for her benefit and I felt cheated not to be able to make use of it.

I rang her flat at teatime. There was no reply so I went to the hospital library and sat in an alcove under the bust of Jenner trying to make sense of a book on strokes. There was a lot of academic guff about which specific problems were caused by damage to which part of the brain, but there's no treatment, so what does it matter? It strikes me that if medical textbooks confined themselves to essential information you could cover the whole subject in about a hundred pages.

Outside the lights from the medical wards were lancing through the orchard. I could see porters and orderlies and technicians shuttling between the hospital and the labs. I closed the textbook and went downstairs to eat.

There was no one I knew in the dining room. I ate some moussaka, then went back to the doctors' residence where Gareth and Kassim and some others were watching a sports program.

Kassim said, "Simon, I hear you're keen on acting."

"Who told you that?"

"A friend of mine in Exeter, Andrew Duncan."

"How does he know?"

"He was at University the same time as you."

"I don't remember him."

"Well, do you still perform?"

"No," I said and left. I walked back through the hospital and down through the terraced grounds to the arbor that overlooked the Avon basin. It was nine o'clock. I went back to my room, picked up my jacket and went to see Christine.

She answered the door wearing a heavy jacket.

"Simon?"

"I was passing and I thought I'd drop in," I said.

"Hi! Come in. I've just got back."

"Where have you been?" I asked.

"London." She rummaged in her pocket for a tissue and blew her nose. "What did you do for the weekend?"

"I was in Cambridge. Reliving the past."

"Ah, yes, the past."

It was difficult to see her face in the half light but there was something in her voice, or maybe in the way she sniffed, then bravely tilted her chin forward that made me suspect she'd been crying.

I turned, and the smile she gave me was too quick and too brief.

"It's cold in here, isn't it? I've been trying to light a fire."

There were some logs and rolled-up newspapers in the grate so I hunkered down and rearranged them and, eventually, the kindling took light.

"Wine or tea?" she asked.

"Wine," I said. "What were you doing in London?"

"Seeing an old friend."

"Is that what the letter was about?"

"Oh, yes, that, yes," she said.

I blew on the flames and the logs began to take. On her way out she put a Ry Cooder record on the turntable. She came back with a bottle of red wine and two glasses. When I took it from her I noticed the ball of tissue crumpled in the ball of her hand.

She laughed and threw it on the fire.

"The ball of tissue paper," she said. It was a joke between us that half the women in the hospital hold a crumpled toilet tissue in their right hand. Whenever you examined them there it would be, like a talisman. "Tell me about Cambridge."

"What do you want to know?" I asked.

"Who did you stay with?"

"A mate of mine. He's called Geoffrey Walker."

"What does he do?"

"He's doing a Ph.D."

"On what?"

"A composer called Gesualdo."

"Never heard of him."

"He's Italian, sixteenth century. He composed madrigals and had a penchant for tying up small boys."

She smiled at that, as I had. "What did you do?"

"On Friday night we went to a party. On Saturday we went horse riding down near Saffron Walden. Then we had a pub meal at the Three Bells on Trumpington Street and went for a moonlight punt down the Cam."

This sounded so good I was almost convinced by it

myself. It struck me, not for the first time, how little solid information is required to fuel a lie.

"What about you?"

"Oh . . ." she said and played with her fingers.

"You don't have to talk about it."

"No, I'm just being silly. It's my Uncle Jack. He's got cancer."

"My God. When did he find out?"

"He's known for months but he just carried on normally. I think that's partly what's so upsetting. This person you think you know so well, then suddenly you find out there's this huge secret he's been keeping from you."

"He was probably just trying not to upset you."

"Yes, I know. It's incredible, isn't it, to have so much strength? All this time I've been writing to him about my stupid little problems and he sends back these wonderful thoughtful replies and then you find that all along . . ." Her voice trailed off.

"What kind of cancer does he have?" I asked.

"Prostate," she said. "And now he's got secondaries in his pelvis and he has to go into a hospice and he won't see anyone or write to anyone anymore and he says he's just going to stay there and die and he won't receive any visitors, not even me."

Her voice quavered on that. She looked at me for a few seconds willing herself not to cry, then covered her face with her hands and sat quaking with her elbows on her knees.

"I'm sure he'll change his mind," I said.

"No, he won't. I went there but they wouldn't let me see him. He's made up his mind he doesn't want any sympathy. He just wants to die alone." Then another wave of pity swept over her and she began weeping aloud.

"Tell me about him," I said softly, but she was crying too much to answer.

After a while, she looked up and said, "I'm sorry . . .

I'm so-sor-sorry," then started sobbing uncontrollably again.

I sat, stranded, watching her. Before the weekend I wouldn't have attempted to comfort her but things were different now. She had opened herself to me.

Also I was still glowing from my discovery of Cambridge. In the past I've been scared of intimacy out of lack of affection for myself. Now, charged with my recently inherited past I discovered new reserves of self-confidence. I crossed the gulf between us and sat beside her.

"Don't cry," I said.

But she continued to. From between her fingers seeped fragments of speech: "It happened so suddenly . . . they said he'd only have another couple of months . . . he has to have morphine for the pain now."

With my left arm I pulled her awkwardly to my side. She tipped toward me and put her arms around my neck. I patted her impotently with my right hand and felt her breasts brush against my arm.

"I'm sorry," she kept saying. "I feel such a fool."

"Don't cry," I said again. "I think you're wonderful." I lifted her face up, meaning to dry her eyes and smile at her but suddenly we were kissing and the hair that had been falling in her eyes was falling into mine and the tears that were streaming down her cheeks were plastered on mine and her arms were wound round my neck and mine around her waist, touching the creamy flesh where her blouse had rucked. I was saying all sorts of things, how I was crazy about her, how I'd wanted her from the first moment we'd met, how beautiful she was. And she was still crying and licking away the tears from her own mouth and it was like that, locked in that first desperate embrace, that we rolled onto the rug. My elbow banged on the floor and she bumped her head and for a moment the confusion cleared and I was looking at very close range into her startled, tear-stained face, feeling bruised and uncomfortable and aroused.

"Oh hell," she said.

"Did you bang your head?"

"Not very much," she laughed breathlessly.

I turned over so she was lying astride one of my legs. A drip had gathered on the end of her nose.

"I hardly know you."

"You don't know me at all," I told her.

"It wouldn't help if I did. I've always been a terrible judge of character."

"Come to bed," I said.

She didn't answer immediately but walked away on bare feet, still sniffing and wiping her nose with her hand, to switch out the light at the far end of the room.

She came back, unbuttoning her dress.

Why is undressing in front of someone so much more embarrassing than actually making love? Is it the lack of choreography? We stepped out of our clothes trembling and uncoordinated, fumbling with laces and buttons, then raced under the quilt, starved and shivering for the feel of flesh on flesh.

"This is madness," she said as we drew together. "I never sleep with people I work with."

"Eysenck says they make the best partners."

"Eysenck's a chauvinist pig."

Then her mouth was on mine and her beautiful legs coiled around and between mine and our bodies pressed together as if trying to cover and conceal every fragment of naked skin. Her hands and slender arms, her legs and belly and breasts and armpits, her tousled scented hair.

"Talk to me," she said.

"What do you want me to say?"

"Say anything." She was nuzzling her head into my shoulder and stroking my chest.

"I'm not a doctor," I told her. "My name's not Simon Hennessey."

She smiled and kissed me, rubbing her pubic hair against my thigh.

"Tell me more," she breathed.

"I never got a degree. I failed first-year biology. I've been a drifter for years. I worked on a kibbutz. I sold vacuum cleaners. I was in therapy for a bit. I worked as a bus conductor . . ."

"Prove it."

"Ask me how many fare stages between Waterloo and The Angel."

"Go on then."

"Twelve."

"You're a very . . . funny . . . person." She punctuated the words with kisses.

"I'm not joking. Its true. My father was a lawyer. My mother has a ceramic shop down the Portobello Road."

"What's it called?"

I could feel her becoming moist. "Handle with Care," I said.

She laughed, holding herself above me. I licked her breasts.

"What's your real name?" she asked.

"Matthew Harris."

Her breathing deepened and she pressed her pelvis down on mine. "Lies turn me on," she whispered. "Come inside me."

CHAPTER
22

NEVER UNDERESTIMATE THE BONDING POWER OF sex—I
went to bed with a relative stranger and woke up unable
to live without her.

We made love in the small hours of the morning—
waking together about four o'clock with my face pressed
against the nape of her neck and her soft buttocks moving sleepily against my cock. And again in the morning,
smiling, kissing, tracing each other's faces with our fingers. Seized with a childish desire to amuse her I came
within a hair's breadth of telling her the truth again but
instead I got up and made coffee in one of those Italian
metal coffeepots. Standing up, half dressed, back in the
real world, we were both self-conscious again. She made
herself busy poaching eggs. I sat at the kitchen table
watching the play of the light on her printed nightgown.

"Feeling better?" I asked.

"Yes."

"I love you."

"You can't say that," she said, bringing the plates to the table.

"Why not?"

"We're still strangers."

"We just slept together."

"Strangers sleep together."

"No, love is measured in honesty."

"Can't strangers be in love?"

"Where's that a quote from?"

The toast sprang up and she brought it to the table. "I don't know," she said. "I read it somewhere. It's true in a way. I knew it was ending with Justin when we started lying to each other."

"Who's Justin?"

She faltered, "An old boyfriend."

I looked across the room for the photo of the man with the beard but it had disappeared.

"And I've . . . liked . . . you, Dr. Hennessey, ever since the second evening we worked together."

"Why?"

"Because you were so straight with me."

I smiled. I was probably the least straight person she'd ever met. I gave her a hug round the back of her chair. "I have to go to work," I said.

Of course, in a logical world getting involved with Christine was the last thing I should have contemplated. I found it difficult enough to maintain credibility in front of casual acquaintances like the Mountfords. It was lunacy to expose myself to a lover's scrutiny. On the other hand, during that spring and early summer in Bristol I wasn't living in a logical world. I was living in a fantasy where my past could be tailored to order and the realization of dreams was an everyday event. I felt capable of anything.

The sun was shining as I left the flat and fine skeins of mist were trailing off the trees that lined the Gorge. Round the back of the hospital there were little green buds peppering the orchard. I walked over to the Accident Department and took over from Hillary. "There's a kidney stone waiting for the urologists," she said. "I've not given him any analgesia yet. We're expecting a fractured neck of femur and there's a foot waiting for X-ray. You're looking pleased with yourself."

"Am I?" It always disturbed me to be reminded of my own transparency.

"Who's the lucky girl, nudge nudge?"

"I'm living like a monk here."

Hillary laughed delightedly. If she hadn't had quite such a vigorous manner she might have been more attractive. "Molly told Gareth you were out all night."

"It's none of Molly's business."

"She's a witch, she finds out everything."

I put on my white coat and picked up the casualty cards. Sunlight was scintillating off the glass fronts of the bookcases and the gardens outside were a riot of daffodils.

"No, she doesn't," I said.

My newfound confidence was largely but not entirely attributable to Christine. At work I'd reached the point where I'd dealt with most common emergencies at least once already. I knew how to fill in the forms. I knew what extensions to ring for help and advice. I knew most of the SHOs by their first names and had grasped enough jargon to talk to them without faltering. I could put up drips and take blood and sew up wounds. I could recite the list of stock questions backward and could recognize a normal chest X ray. These are simple skills. They had

taken me two months to learn, which is just about the
length of time it takes for any rookie doctor, and during
the period I was learning them I was no more dangerous
than the flood of new medical graduates who hit the hospitals of Britain every autumn.

What's ironic was that most of the most difficult bits
of business, like the wrist movement required for drumming on the back of people's chests, turned out to be
completely useless. You're supposed to be able to tell
from this whether someone's lungs are congested, but it
struck me fairly early on that it's an archaic piece of nonsense. A chest X ray tells you far more than any amount
of drumming. It seems to me there's a conspiracy of the-
atricality running through the profession. If chest percussion is a sham, then somebody should say so and save
everyone a lot of time. Still, no one likes to criticize the
emperor's clothes; I certainly wasn't about to risk it.

Christine and I spent all our free time together, talking,
making love, exchanging confidences. Love and honesty
may be inextricably linked but it was several weeks before
Christine penetrated the surface and realized how little of
myself I was revealing to her.

We spent a lot of our free time roaring around in the
Triumph together, Christine with her hand on my thigh
laughing and singing and yelling to me over the noise of
the wind.

One day she took me to see the spa in Bath. We sat on a
stone bench listening to the footsteps of visitors echoing
over the flagstones and watching steam rising off the turquoise waters. She said, "Do you think people can
change?"

"Change in what way?"

"I mean, suppose you're one sort of person and you

want to be a different sort of person, do you think you can do that?"

"I think it would be very difficult," I said.

"Have you never tried to do it?" she asked.

"No."

"I have," she said.

Some American tourists were doing a tour of the baths. We could hear the guide's voice echoing over the flagstones from the direction of the steam room.

"What sort of person do you want to be?"

"Better," she said.

"Better in what way?"

"Morally, spiritually."

I kissed her and felt her slim waist through her pullover.

"Physically you're perfect," I said.

"Sometimes I don't think it's possible," she said. "Sometimes I think you're born with the germ of a personality and everything you do—in your family, at school and afterward—is all just variations on a theme."

"I know someone who changed," I said.

"How did they do it?"

"They moved to a different city. They took an entirely different job and cut off all contact with their past."

"Did it make them a better person?"

"It made them happier," I said. "That probably makes them better."

"How long did they last?"

"How do you mean?"

"I mean before they went back to their old ways?"

"I don't think they'll ever go back."

"I think they will," she said. "Everyone goes back."

I thought about Alec and wondered if he was still trapped in the West Harwood. Had I escaped or was I still on the run?

"I'm sorry," she said. "I didn't mean to depress you."

I said, "I thought we were talking about you."

*   *   *

The following weekend she went to London and came back to report that her uncle was in reasonable health and had agreed to carry on seeing her. After that she continued to visit him on a regular basis, arranged to coincide with my weekends on call. I suppose I might have resented her relationship with the old buffer but in fact I found it rather touching. She didn't talk about him much and I didn't ask. It was part of her mystery.

Going to the Spa on Sundays also became a regular event. Afterward we'd sit in Cathedral Square having breakfast outside the Italian coffee shop. We'd buy a pile of Sunday papers and Christine would read the world news while I flicked through the color supplements. I can remember her snatching them away from me and flicking through them saying, "How can you read this stuff? It's worthless. It's pandering to the worst possible instincts—greed, envy, the cult of the personality. I mean, look at this nonsense—who are these people? Teenage pinups, soap-opera stars. What the hell have they ever done for anyone? This is irrelevant. It's not worth your time."

Then she would go back to reading about famine and pollution with an expression of beatific intensity.

I think back to April and I think of drinking in the Watershed and walks in Leigh Woods and feeding the deer in Ashton Court. I think of mornings cuddled up under Christine's pink quilt, and getting lost in Somerset lanes and driving home with flagons of cider in the backseat. For that month alone the rest was almost worth it.

Christine didn't like to mix socially with the other doctors, which suited me fine—I couldn't afford the risk. It was much safer to socialize with her nonmedical

friends. Some nights we would go down to the old cobbled wharves and drink in the Duke where fat men with
well-trimmed beards played jazz every night. Or go danc-
ing at the Dug Out, a basement discotheque near the university, which was always as dark as Africa and thick with
the scent of marijuana.

The only fly in the ointment was Molly.

I'd always patronized the dwarf less than the other
doctors. I didn't owe her anything and I couldn't see how
she'd be much use to me except for providing the sweet
tea which I routinely poured down the sink. But our relationship was fairly stress-free until Christine slept in my
room. In the morning Molly barged in as usual. It wasn't
till she'd set the coffee on the bedside table that she realized there were two of us. I woke up with a start to see
her crumpled face inches from my own. She snorted and
stumped away, bandy-legged, arms akimbo, slamming the
door behind her with surprising force.

Christine wanted to go and apologize. Personally I
didn't see why. The dwarf was just the housekeeper and
if she didn't approve of people sleeping together that was
her problem, not mine. But Christine still felt bad about it
so I said I'd have a word.

I found Molly in the residence kitchen, standing on a
stool to wash some pans. She ignored me when I came in.

"Molly?"

"What be you wanting?"

"I'm sorry if I offended you."

"Rules is rules," she said.

"I didn't know there were any rules."

"Well, that's because you don't never ask. Maybe you
should talk to people."

"Really, Molly, I don't think it's anybody else's business what I do with my private life."

"It's my business. Someone's got to clean the sheets,
don't they?"

"Well, I'll clean them myself," I said.

She crashed some pans about. She needed both hands to lift the bottle of detergent. "It's not a matter of that. It's a matter of what I say goes. You just don't want to fit in, do you?"

"We're consenting adults."

"Not in my house, you're not. You want to do that you go and do it elsewhere."

"Fair enough," I said, turning to leave.

"You're an odd one," she said darkly. "And so is she. I know about the pair of you. I watch and I listen."

"Well, I'd be grateful if you wouldn't."

"I'm sure you would," she said.

I told Hillary what had happened and she suggested I buy Molly some flowers. I considered this and decided against it. I wasn't going to be intimidated by the midget. Let her stew. What did I have to worry about? I had an income of £12,000 a year. I had a beautiful girlfriend and the name Dr. Simon Hennessey on my checkbook. I still couldn't believe my own good fortune. The whole thing had the two-dimensional quality of a film. In fact, the romance was probably heightened by its fragility. I knew that one day it could all fall apart—that pulling one loose thread might destroy the whole artificial image. And indeed, the first argument I ever had with Christine created a rent in the fabric more irreparable than anything I could have imagined.

CHAPTER 23

22nd April

Hello Matthew,
Message in a bottle this one. Sent you a card a month ago but got no reply. Don't imagine the poste restante on St. Lucia is too reliable.

Was impressed by your just taking off like that. When it comes to the crunch not many people can make the break. Hope you didn't get seasick.

Getting hacked off with portering myself & thinking of enrolling as a nurse—don't laugh—I look dead good in white. Two-year course. Crying out for applicants.

Money's piss awful but that's not the important thing, is it? (Don't say yes.) Always fancied working in a refugee camp. Plan is to do the old training, then scoot. World's a big place but we could meet up. You never know.

Anyway, chances are you'll never read this and it'll just gather dust in some West Indian office till someone opens it to see if there's any money inside.

Here's to us, Wha's like us.

Your old pal,
Alec

CHAPTER 24

MY LUCK RAN OUT ON THE first of May. May Day. Ha. Very appropriate.

Another perfect morning. In the tennis court at the center of the hospital two orderlies were erecting the net. I walked over to the doctors' residence to pick up my stuff and found Molly cleaning my room.

"I don't know why you bother coming back here," she said.

"I live here, Molly."

"You wouldn't know it."

"Molly, you didn't want us sleeping here together. What option do I have?"

"You could give up seeing that girl. Keep your work and socializing separate."

"Really, it's none of your business."

"You'll regret it. Mark my words," she said. I went across to the dining room for brunch, where I met Hillary.

"Working with the wife this afternoon," she said.

"She's not my wife," I said.

"Just teasing."

"I don't know why everyone makes such a big deal about it."

"I wasn't criticizing," said Hillary. "I'm full of admiration for you. I think I'd find it very difficult to work with my boyfriend."

"You get used to it," I said.

In fact, the converse was true. When I'd first started I depended on the way Christine tended to take control at work. Now, more and more I found myself resenting it. I was the doctor after all. I should be making the decisions.

Both Molly and Hillary had sensitized me to this and that afternoon I started deliberately changing my mind or asking Christine to do things in a way she wasn't used to. She didn't say anything in front of the patients but as soon as we had a lull she tidied up with a clanging display of efficiency and went off to roll bandages without speaking to me. Anyway, that's why she wasn't around when Celia Mountford came in.

I heard her before I saw her.

"Simon, it's you. I'm so glad."

She was impeccably dressed in high-heeled shoes and a camel-colored mohair suit but her hair was slightly disarrayed and her face rather pale. She wore her jacket over her shoulders. Underneath it her arm was in a sling made from a black and white Hermès scarf. I asked what had happened and she sat down, smiling and shaking her head.

"It's so silly, really. I'd been visiting a friend of mine ... she's just bought a new shop—antique prints, and this was drinks to celebrate the opening night ..."

As she spoke she was trying to shrug the jacket off her shoulders. I helped her with it and hung it on the back of the door.

She caught sight of her reflection in the window and smoothed her hair with her left hand.

". . . Anyway I'd just got in the front door and the carpet has come up from that metal whatsit—you know— so over I went on this wrist." She laughed at this but her arm was resting on her lap and the movement obviously hurt her.

I leaned over her to untie the sling.

"Is Ben . . . is Dr. Mountford outside?" I asked.

"No—he's at a symposium in Sheffield."

"Maybe I should ring Dr. Thorn."

"Oh, no, don't do that," she said quickly, and I remembered the story about how he'd saved her husband's job. Maybe she didn't like being beholden to him. Maybe she just didn't like him—I could understand that.

"All right," I said. "Let's have a look at you."

"It's just a sprain, isn't it? It's a bit swollen though. I really just came for a bandage."

I pressed gently on the wrist and she winced. There was an obvious step in the bone.

"No," I said. "It's a Colles' fracture." I delivered this with a blasé air of experience, secretly proud of having remembered the correct name. I packed her off to X-ray and went through to the plaster room. A Colles' fracture was the first problem I'd dealt with in this department— that first night before I'd officially started work. I'd seen two pulled straight since then and it seemed pretty simple. I was ready to do one myself. It would be quite a coup to fix up the consultant's wife. Mountford would be effusively grateful and it might even impress Thorn. I didn't want Christine stealing my thunder so I checked out the equipment myself.

The blood-pressure cuffs were hanging on the wall. I filled a basin with lukewarm water and looked out some plaster of Paris and a padding roll. By the time I'd got it all together Celia Mountford was out of X-ray.

I wheeled her out of the plaster room and got her to sit up on the trolley—she looked rather out of place sitting on her own in the middle of all that white tiling—like a duchess doing a tour of an abattoir. I helped her off with her blouse. She was wearing a pink silk shift out of which her plump freckled breasts rose with each breath. Thirty years earlier she would have been pretty sexy. They tell you that doctors don't get a kick out of undressing their patients but this has got to be bullshit. I often felt mildly turned on. It was one of the perks of the job.

I wrapped the funeral black cuff around her arm.

"I'm going to inject the back of your hand with some local anesthetic."

"As long as you know what you're doing." She said it with a twinkle, assuming that I did. I put the butterfly needle in a vein, wondering as I did so what the dose of Marcaine was—three vials diluted in two of saline or two diluted in three. I didn't want to go and look it up in case I ran into Christine so I opted for the higher dose. The last thing I wanted was for the arm not to be numb when I pulled the fracture straight.

"I suppose you do quite a lot of these," she said.

"Quite a few."

I was filling the 50 cc syringe. It looked like a hell of a lot.

"Tell me what you've been up to," I said, fitting it to the bung at her wrist.

"Oh, the usual. Gardening, pottering about. I put a lot of honeysuckle up the back fence yesterday."

I smiled and nodded. I was having to press pretty hard on the plunger but, gradually, it was going in.

"How does that feel?"

"Cold . . . tingly."

"That's the way."

I heard footsteps in the corridor outside and saw Christine walk past. She didn't see me. A minute later she came back again, looking down, presumably holding a cup of coffee.

I checked the syringe; 40 ccs had gone in. As I remembered it the veins of the arm were supposed to stand out and the skin go white and mottled. This wasn't actually happening. I squirted in the last 10 ccs.

"How does that feel?"

"I feel a bit sick."

"Yes, that's normal."

It wasn't normal. Nothing was normal. I wondered where I'd gone wrong. I dropped the syringe in the bucket at my feet and touched the fracture. "Is it numb yet?"

"No—I don't think so."

I pressed on the fracture and she winced. Her pulse was OK. She did look a bit on the pale side but I reckoned it was just the pain.

"We'll leave it for a moment, shall we?" I said.

I turned away to cut the plaster. My lips were dry but I managed to whistle a few bars of "On the Street Where You Live," imagining how afterward she'd tell Mountford how confident and efficient I'd been. There was still time to call Christine to come and help but I knew that if I called her in now she'd be annoyed at me for not getting hold of her at the beginning. I made a slab of plaster about nine inches long and cut a notch for Celia Mountford's thumb.

"I think I'm going to be sick," she said.

"Not to worry."

I looked at her face. She didn't look well at all. A glossy bloom of sweat had sprung out from her forehead. "You're doing just fine," I said.

As I spoke I realized my mistake—the cuff! I'd put the cuff on her arm but I hadn't inflated it. You were supposed to pump it up to stop the anesthetic from trav-

eling any farther than the arm veins. I'd left it loosely tied
and shot the whole dose of Marcaine directly into her system.

"Oh, help," she said weakly.

My hands skittered over the valves. I found the rubber bulb and pumped till the cuff was ballooning round
her upper arm. The veins filled up and the site where I'd
put the needle began to ooze dark blood. I picked up her
other wrist. Her hand was cold and clammy. The only
pulse I could feel was my own racing heartbeat.

"All right," I said. "That's good. That all seems fine."

I went back to her broken wrist, intending, whether
it was anesthetized or not, to pull the bloody thing
straight and get it over with.

I held her elbow with one hand and yanked on her
fingers with the other. Nothing happened. It had looked
pretty simple when Adam did it. At least Celia didn't cry
out—maybe the anesthetic was working. I gave it another
tug and she slumped heavily toward me.

"That's the way," I said, sweating. "Not too sore?"

She didn't answer. I glanced at her and time
stopped.

Her eyes had rolled toward the ceiling. Her mouth
had flopped open and her tongue was protruding slightly
between her teeth. The color had completely drained
from her face, making her lipstick look clumsy and inap-
propriate. She wasn't breathing.

"Celia? Mrs. Mountford?"

I slapped her and her head lolled sideways. I whim-
pered and clutched at the crotch of my trousers. "Celia!"

Her lips were tinged with blue now and her tongue
seemed to be growing inside her mouth like an obscene
purple tumor. I went round the other side of her, my
leather soles slipping on the wet tiled floor. I knocked
against the stainless-steel trolley and it careered across the
floor into the equipment cabinet.

"Celia?"

I hit her on the chest. My fist landed with a spongy thud. Nothing changed—her blue tongue continued to protrude and her fishy eyes to stare heavenward. I flailed around blindly for the oxygen and saw it attached to a nearby wall. I turned it on full and began trying to untangle the twisted black tubing. When I got it straight it wouldn't reach her.

I tried to push her trolley toward the wall and it wouldn't move. The brakes were locked on so I had to heave it screaming across the floor, leaving black scars of rubber on the white tiles. When it reached the wall the back of the trolley collapsed and Celia fell back with a crash, one lifeless arm sweeping laryngoscopes and endotracheal tubes of the stainless-steel shelf.

You die three minutes after you stop breathing and I don't know how much of Celia Mountford's time I used up then—everything I did seemed to take forever. When I picked up the oxygen mask I was shaking so much it seemed to twitch and convulse like a hideous sea insect. I clamped it over her face.

How long did I stand there with the hissing mask obscuring her face and my thighs vibrating against the sides of the trolley? Five seconds? Five minutes? My mind was racing frantically, purposelessly, like the wheels of a car stuck in sand. Ludicrous, unrelated images chased through my head—the pattern on Christine's quilt. Thorn in his office, Mountford's grandfather, the bridge at night . . . They say that when you drown your whole life flashes before your eyes but what they must mean is this furious mental overdrive that accompanies the final stages of panic.

I waded from the trolley to the swing doors, flung them open and bellowed Christine's name down the glittering corridor.

I let the door swing back and hurried back to Celia Mountford. The black oxygen bag was tense as a football and the useless gas was still leaking out between the mask and her face. I pushed up and down on her ribs but couldn't persuade her to breathe. I could hear Christine coming up the corridor at what seemed a ridiculously leisurely pace. She opened the door and stood there for a few moments taking in the scene: the bowl of water, the plaster of Paris, the woman with an oxygen mask over her face, and myself, standing slack with horror in the midst of it all.

"What are you doing?" she asked.

"Ring two-seven-seven."

"What's happened? Who is it?"

"She's arrested. Hurry!"

"Who's arrested?"

"Just phone, will you, for Christ's sakes!"

I saw a shadow pass over her face, then she turned quickly to the phone. As she dialed I made a feeble attempt at external cardiac massage but the trolley was too high for me to get much downward pressure.

"Here, I'll do that."

Christine dragged up a steel step and pushed me out of the way. She pressed three or four times, then lifted the mask off.

"Hail, Mary, full of grace."

Until then I had never seen Christine panicking. Her eyes filled with tears. "Oh my God, oh dear God," she said. She pulled Celia's chin forward and put the mask back on. When she pressed the demand valve, Celia's chest started to move.

"It's Celia Mountford!"

I nodded dumbly. The skin of my face felt stretched unbearably tight.

"How did she get here? When did she come in? What have you been doing?"

I had lost the power of speech. Christine was pumping on Celia's chest, then squeezing the oxygen-demand valve. Four pumps, then a breath. Four pumps, then a breath. Her hair was falling over her face and the trolley was creaking and rattling with her exertions.

"Get a drip in then."

I hauled myself out of the stupor that had overtaken me and started looking for needles despite an overwhelming sense of futility. I'd seen Gough and others since him dragged back from the brink of death but you learn to recognize the point of no return and Celia Mountford was past it.

Then suddenly the swing doors were crashing open and the arrest team was there armed with serious efficiency and trolleys of equipment—the curved Perspex tube they stuffed down her throat, the huge preloaded syringes and the six-inch cardiac needles.

I stood silent and waited as they cut off her silk slip and positioned the greasy defib paddles on her chest and twice, three times, four times galvanized her white corpse into a parody of the death spasm. I'd seen lots of unsuccessful resuscitation attempts but this one was different, allegorical, a brutal tableau of the murder I'd already committed.

CHAPTER 25

THEY HAD GIVEN UP AFTER HALF an hour. The floor was strewn with discarded giving sets, sterile paper wrappers, syringes and needles. Two orderlies, the lucky bastards, were winding up the ECG leads and repacking the trolley. The anesthetist was clipping up her plastic case. The body of Celia Mountford lay dead on the trolley, naked from the waist. Hammond, the resident, was writing the resuscitation report in his small, neat hand.

"So what happened? Did the cuff deflate?"

"I guess so."

"Was it leaking?"

"It must have been," I told him.

He pulled a face and then went back to his notes. "And you called us immediately?"

"Yes."

*   *   *

The orderlies left, followed by the anesthetist. Celia Mountford's body lay with the sheet pulled over it.

"Did the cuff deflate?"

"I guess so."

This exchange flickered like a candle through the fog of panic and confusion. He had offered the excuse so casually that there had to be a precedent. It had never even occurred to him that the cuff wasn't pumped up in the first place. I walked over to Celia Mountford's body and pulled the sheet back from her face. Her mouth was open but her eyes were closed. I took a large, bloody needle off the stainless-steel trolley and followed the sphygmomanometer tube down to the cuff at her arm. The limbs of a dead person seem twice as heavy as they are in life. I picked up Celia Mountford's arm and made a hole in the blood-pressure cuff, near the seam. In retrospect it seems like the act of a cool and rational man but at the time I was almost incapable of holding the needle. I was no more conscious of obscuring the trail than a hunted fox who doubles back through the stream. The crisis had stripped me of all humanity. I was responding as an animal.

After it was finished I walked out into the corridor and let the swing doors flap shut behind me. I didn't have the strength to release them gently. I felt pulled and battered and stretched and wrung out. I wanted to curl up in some dark and secret place and weep, I wanted to disappear, I wanted to wind back time. But in the bright, unforgiving light of the Casualty Department none of these things was possible. I waited outside the plaster room, wondering if there was anything else that might betray my incompetence but I found now that I couldn't go back in there. Instead I wandered around past the empty cubicles to the doctors' room.

Christine was on the phone. "The Royal Hotel," she was saying, "outside Birmingham."

She held me in her gaze—a look of profound religious sadness. I sat down and studied the floor.

"Hello. Royal Hotel? Yes. Dr. Benjamin Mountford. He's one of the delegates."

I looked at my watch—half past twelve already. The last thing I remembered clearly was Celia Mountford arriving three hours previously. It seemed less than a heartbeat ago.

Now I pictured Mountford sleeping in green silk pajamas in a hotel room with wooden veneer on the bedhead and a jug of water with a plastic seal on top. I pictured him waking, groping for the light switch, consulting the traveling clock and reaching for the phone.

"Dr. Mountford? It's Christine here from the Casualty Department. . . . There's been a terrible accident. . . ."

I could hear, across the miles of wire, the thin, high sound of Mountford's voice. "Yes?"

"It's your wife," said Christine.

"Yes . . . an accident you say . . . involving Celia . . . Hello . . . is she all right? . . . Hello?"

"I'm afraid she's dead," said Christine softly—too softly because at first Mountford thought he'd misheard and I could hear him, wide awake now and saying frantically, "Hello . . . Come again . . . Yes? . . . What happened? . . . Hello?"

"She's dead. Celia's dead."

"Oh my . . . She can't be . . . Are you sure?"

"Sure." Christine choked and swallowed. "Quite sure."

An interminable silence on the other end of the line. Christine still regarding me with those desperate eyes from which now two tears began flowing down her face. She made no effort to stop them. The gray rivulets of mascara gathered under her chin and dripped into the mouthpiece of the receiver.

"Come again," Mountford said at last. "Come again, what happened?"

"It was . . . a . . ." Christine seemed lost, out of breath ". . . a broken wrist—something with the anesthetic."

"Hello . . . Come again . . . Hello . . . What?"

"Speak to Dr. Hennessey." She crammed the slippery receiver into my hand and rushed from the room. I was left speechless and fumbling.

"Hello," he was saying. "Hello?"

"This is Simon," I said.

"Simon who?"

"Dr. Hennessey."

"Oh, yes . . . hello . . . what's this about Celia?"

"She's dead," I said. "Celia's dead. She was having a Bier's block for a Colles' fracture. The cuff deflated and the Marcaine injection stopped her heart. We tried to revive her for half an hour but it was too late. I'm . . . we're all terribly sorry."

"Was it you?" he asked. "Were you looking after her?"

"The equipment was faulty, Dr. Mountford. The cuff was leaking. It all happened very quickly."

"Who was in charge?"

"There was nothing we could do," I said.

There was another long silence in which I began to hear a plaintiff high-pitched sound like a chained dog. Down the corridor Christine came out of the bathroom, her face inhumanly white.

On the phone Mountford stopped crying. "I'll try and get down tonight," he said.

"How will you do that?"

"I don't know. Can one hire a car?"

I said, "Stay till morning. There's nothing to be done." Then I hung up, Christine sat down still staring at me. Somewhere down the corridor one of the orderlies was playing Radio Two.

"Why didn't you call me?"

"I did call you," I said. "I couldn't find you."

"You knew where I was."

"I didn't know where you were. I called you and you didn't answer. What do you expect me to do? Leave her hanging around with a broken arm while I trail around looking for you?"

"Don't get cross."

"Well, stop trying to make me feel guilty," I said.

"I'm just trying to understand what happened."

"You're trying to establish that it was my fault," I said.

"Who said anything about whose fault it was? What does it matter? I feel terrible—you feel terrible. And poor old Benny Mountford . . ."

I could think of no response to this and she mistook this silence for remorse.

"I'm sorry," she said. "It was just as much me. I shouldn't have left you like that."

"Just forget it," I said. "I don't want to talk about it."

"I'm just trying to be supportive."

"I don't want support, Christine. I just need to think. OK?"

I stood up. Her wet, dark eyes were making me feel edgy. "It doesn't move you, does it?" she said. "You don't care about Celia. You didn't really feel sorry for Mountford—embarrassed but not sorry—I don't think you're capable of pity."

I said, "You don't know what I feel."

"I think I do."

"OK then," I said, "I'm not sorry for Celia Mountford. Or her husband. I hardly knew them. If you want to know what I feel now it's fear. At least I don't try to disguise it with a load of bogus piety."

There was a moment in which I could have retracted that last outburst but I didn't. Instead I said, "I'm going to bed," and went off to the on-call room, leaving her slight figure alone in the doctors' room.

The on-call room was like a cell—white and windowless with a small cot in the corner. I hung up my coat and took a shower, standing under it long after I was clean, letting the warm spray beat against my skin. I could run but how far would I get? Running was as good as a confession of murder. If I stayed, there would be some kind of an inquiry—I had no doubt about that but there remained a chance, however slight, that I might evade justice. Christine, with her Catholic facility for guilt, was already preparing to shoulder a part of the blame and I remembered also how Celia Mountford had said (it seemed years ago now that she was a living, breathing person) that her husband was responsible for the maintenance of equipment. Maybe I could unload some guilt onto him.

Christine was right of course. This fever of self-preservation was despicable and if I had any capacity for love and morality I should have given myself up to Thorn. But love and morality exist most of the time only in theory and when they emerge into the concrete world they are bloody difficult to grasp. Shame I understand. Guilt I understand. Heroism?—I think it's an aberration, a communal myth, and what we interpret as heroic acts are mostly accidents of circumstance. The moral majority don't believe this, but the trouble with the moral majority is they've never been there. They don't know what it's like to feel the knife hovering at the base of your skull. You can imagine how you'd act. But you don't know.

I know. And I blame no one—cowards, liars, cheats, torturers, murderers, deserters . . . I was that soldier.

I dried myself, shivering. I couldn't even find it in myself to go back and comfort Christine. My confidence was shot—there were so many imponderables. What could they find from a postmortem on Celia? Would Christine turn against me? Could they tell that the cuff had been sabotaged? These questions lodged, like a physical mass, in the dark on the edge of my bed, trying unsuccessfully to digest them.

CHAPTER
26

2nd May

Dear J,
The worst thing has happened. I feel I've killed some-
one. I was working with Simon and getting cross with
him—he'd started behaving like the rest of them—all
self-important and autocratic. You know how much
that enrages me. You of all people know that.

So I just retreated and let him get on with it, just
walked off the set. And while I was indulging myself in
this stupid schoolgirl huff the wife of the consultant
came in with a broken arm, and Simon had to deal
with it himself and she died. A bit of the equipment
went wrong. I should have been looking after it.

Every day you deal with people dying you think

*you're being fantastically sympathetic. But you're not—
it's all sham. I know that now. I saw Celia Mountford
dead and it was just a totally different dimension. Suddenly I was dealing with real life. So what has it been
all the rest of the time?*

*We argued afterward. I accused Simon of not car-
ing. He said I was just as bad—worse. He called it my
"bogus piety." Maybe he's right. I feel like someone
who's been told the last three years have been a con.
That none of it was real. Maybe it wasn't, I can't tell
anymore.*

*There's going to be an inquest. We had to write
down everything that happened and now we're both
supposed to carry on working. I know how these things
go. Everyone gets asked the routine questions and everyone says how tragic and unavoidable it was and a
ream of notes gets written and we're all expected to go
back to life as normal. It's not normal. It's not normal
for her husband anymore and just now I don't feel
right working here. What am I saying? Maybe I'm just
embarrassed to go back in the hospital. I don't trust any
of my worthy emotions anymore. I look at what I regarded as sacrifice and pity and love and they're just
ways of getting what I want. I spoke to Thorn and told
him I had to go away for a bit and he said OK.*

*I'm coming to London. I need to talk things
through with you. Even when you're being pompous
you make me feel secure.*

Lots of love,
Christine

CHAPTER 27

"Do you need a stamp?"

"What for?"

"The letter you were writing."

"No, I'll post it some other time," she said.

"Where are you going?"

"Church," she said.

"It's Saturday."

"I know."

"You don't want to come for a drive?" I asked her.

"What for?"

So she went off to the church and I went back to the doctors' residence. I called in at the hospital library and picked up a book on local-anesthetic techniques, then I walked back to the residence and locked myself in my room. I sat with the book, trying to memorize, word for word, the correct Bier's block procedure but recently I'd been finding it impossible to concentrate. I envisaged Thorn probing my references and finding a description that didn't tally. I imagined rumors circulating, my name being bandied about, news of the accident seeping back to London. I stood for hours in my room, scared of running, scared of staying, watching with growing alienation the bursting signs of summer in the orchard outside. Lately the phone had been ringing at odd times. Now it rang again. I put on my jacket and went for a drive.

On the way downstairs I met Molly. She obviously knew of the accident because she now greeted me with a cheerful, maternal smile. I scowled at her. I didn't want her sympathy.

I drove over the bridge and went for a walk in Clifton village. Suddenly everyone was wearing summer clothes. I felt out of step in my jeans and thick pullover. They'd changed everything and no one had told me. Christine had been my only real contact with the world and now I was losing her too. I bought a couple of T-shirts and sat in the coffee shop but everyone seemed to be sharing a joke from which I was excluded. I walked down Princess Victoria Street past the painted mews houses. The Avon Gorge Hotel was open so I called in for a drink and stood alone with my pint on the veranda, watching the hospital across the Gorge. Where was Mountford? What was Thorn up to?

"Simon." A hand descended on my shoulder and I almost choked. It was Hillary with one of the other doctors.

"Simon, this is Mike. Mike . . . Simon."

We shook hands.

"Simon's the Casualty Officer."

"Ah, yes." The doctor called Mike sipped his beer. "I've heard . . ."

They both looked to me as though I might want to say something but I didn't.

Hillary shaded her eyes against the sun. She had very pale blue eyes. Her brows and eyelashes were almost invisible. "We're going down to Glastonbury. Do you want to come?"

"No, I've got a couple of things to do."

"Well, if you ever want to talk . . ."

"Thanks," I said and finished my drink.

I left and walked back to the hospital, keeping my eyes down to avoid anyone who might recognize me. The bastards. They all wanted the inside story. I felt like a Moors Murderer.

I got in the car and drove out past Ashton Court and across to Gordano. I parked on the overpass and watched the cars on the M5 rushing south to Exeter and north to Birmingham. Beyond the motorway I could see hills and hedgerows. I could see the Severn Bridge and the water of the estuary. Portishead to the north, Avonmouth to the east. A hundred farms and villages dotting the intervening countryside. There are no open spaces—nowhere to hide anymore—the world isn't big enough. I got in the car and drove back to Bristol.

The warm weather broke and it drizzled obligingly for the funeral. I stayed behind in Christine's flat looking out over the distant glassy waters of the docks. The city was veiled in gray mist from which there emerged, just beyond the water's edge, the stoical red blocks of tobacco warehouses.

Christine came back at three, shaking the water off her hat.

"How was it?"

"Miserable, embarrassing. A lot of sidelong glances—
'*She's the nurse who was there when it happened*—' I stood at
the back and left as soon as it was over."

"It was brave of you to go."

"I'd have felt worse if I hadn't."

She didn't intend that as an accusation but it smarted
like one. "Who was there?" I asked.

"Everybody."

"What did you sing?"

"Anglican hymns—I didn't know them."

"How did you get back?"

"I walked."

Since the morning after the accident all our conversations had that functional, staccato quality. It felt like
trying to fly a kite on a day without wind. I needed her
support. I didn't want to lose her—she was the only comfort left to me. But the wind had dropped and I was left
wondering if it had ever existed. Love, like medicine, de-
pends on faith and illusion; in the crisis I had lost my
grip on both of them. Talking about acting, Christine had
once said, "You must never come out of character—if you
fluff your lines you have to fluff them in character. If you
trip on the carpet trip up in character. The greatest sin
you can commit is to deny that the play is real." That's
what had happened. I'd stopped believing. Maybe we
both had.

"Would you like some tea?"

"Yes, please."

"Your shoes are wet."

"I know."

She arranged them on the radiator as I boiled the
kettle, then she went through to the bathroom and buf-
feted her hair with a towel. She came back wearing a long
woolen jersey. I sat with her and made another clumsy
attempt at reconciliation.

"Chris."

"Yes."

"You know I'm sorry."

"Sorry. Yes. We're both sorry."

"Someday I'll tell you about myself."

"Tell me what?" she asked.

"Oh, skeletons in the cupboard."

She smiled wanly. "It doesn't matter," she said. "It's not important."

"It's important to me."

"OK then."

She was unimpressed, as children are when you offer them something they instinctively know you can't deliver. I'd never be able to share the truth with her.

"Are you definitely going off to London?"

"Yes."

"Will you tell your uncle what happened?"

"I tell him everything."

"You must be very close."

"We are," she said.

I put my arm around her shoulder and we sat solemnly watching the cat nibbling at the spider plant. The position was uncomfortable and I couldn't sustain it for long.

At night we lay in bed wrapped around each other out of custom rather than passion. I made a few exploratory sexual overtures but since the accident neither of us felt particularly turned on. In the morning she left for London.

That evening I was reading in my room at the residence when there was a knock on the door. I unlocked it and found Adam wearing a carefully laundered pale-blue track suit.

"Can I come in?"

I couldn't think of a suitable excuse so I stood aside and let him past.

"Nice room you've got here," he said.

His own was the floor below but I'd never previously invited him up. "You can see the bridge," he said.

"Just when it's lit up."

"What's that building behind the path. labs?"

"The laundry."

He crossed to the mantelpiece and studied Simon's school photograph. "Which one's you?" he asked.

"Third from the right in the top row."

He looked at it, then back to me. "Amazing how people change," he said.

"Do you want to go downstairs for a drink?" I asked.

"No, I had one with Tony Hammond after the game."

"Is there anything I can do for you?"

"No, I just came to see you were OK."

"How do you mean, OK?"

"Well, this inquest hanging over you. It must be very worrying."

"I'm sure it'll be all right," I said.

"Sure, just a formality." He had got the message and had turned back toward the door. "Just so long as you know that we're all supporting you," he said.

"I appreciate that, Adam."

"If you ever fancy a game of squash . . ."

"Thanks," I said.

"When's the inquest?"

"In a couple of weeks now."

"Well," he said, "it could have happened to anyone."

"Yes, sure."

"Good-bye then, Simon."

"Good-bye."

I closed and locked the door behind him. I didn't trust any of them.

*   *   *

The day before the inquest Christine came back, bright
and brittle, wearing a man's dinner jacket she had bought
on the King's Road. In the intervening weeks she had
regained strength and confidence. She seemed more
positive, more decided than I had ever seen her before.
In contrast I felt pale and haunted, ravaged by self-doubt
and by the cancerous effects of secrecy.

CHAPTER
28

"COURT RISE."

We all stood up, Christine and myself in the pews along the side of the room; Mountford, Thorn, the pathologist and most of the others in the rows facing the coroner's bench. The Casualty receptionist was here, and an extravagantly dressed woman with a handkerchief, who I guessed was Celia Mountford's artist friend. Tony Hammond, who'd attempted the resuscitation, was sitting near the back. There were more than two dozen others whom I didn't recognize.

The coroner came in, a brisk, handsome man in a dark suit. His name was Lovejoy. We all sat down again and the policeman who seemed to be orchestrating proceedings said, "Will it please you, sir, to hear the evidence in the case of Mrs. Celia Mountford?"

The coroner nodded and signaled for proceedings to commence.

"Call Dr. Benjamin Mountford."

Old Mountford got up and headed for the witness box. He'd got himself jammed in by two or three people who'd arrived late and sat at the end of his row. There was a lot of inelegant scuffling as he freed himself of them.

"You swear to tell the truth, the whole truth, and nothing but the truth?"

"I do," said Mountford.

One of my legs was already vibrating wildly. I moved along a fraction so Christine wouldn't notice it. There were Gothic windows along the side of the room opposite us. They looked out on to a small paved courtyard, dominated by the blank rear wall of the Bristol Royal Infirmary. It reminded me of a prison exercise yard.

"You are Dr. Benjamin Mountford of Twenty-three Down Road, Bristol?"

"That is correct."

"You last saw your wife alive when?"

"On the morning of the first of May. I was leaving for a conference in Birmingham."

"And when did you learn of her death?"

"Early morning—the second."

Mountford looked thinner and paler than I remembered him, not quite filling the light gray suit. His chubby hands fidgeted on the edges of the witness box and he frequently took his glasses off to polish them. As he answered the questions I looked across to Thorn, sitting ramrod straight and facing the front. His suit jacket was crushed at the elbows and in the armpits. What did he know? Whom had he contacted? Surely if he'd found anything out about me he'd have acted by now. His sculptured profile gave nothing away but somehow he must have sensed me looking at him because he suddenly turned toward me. I looked hurriedly away and pretended to be studying the heraldic shields on the back wall of the room.

"And had your wife previously enjoyed good health?"

"She'd had a hysterectomy, twenty years previously. And she'd recently suffered from paroxysmal atrial tachycardia."

"Can you explain that in layman's terms?"

"It's a minor heart complaint . . . palpitations. . . . It's not serious, not usually."

I saw the court recorder writing this down and made a mental note to incorporate it into my own account of the accident.

They called the artist woman next and she told how Celia had drunk no more than a glass of sherry and had seemed perfectly well when she left the exhibition. She dabbed her eyes and nose a lot when she described this. In the audience I saw Mountford blinking repeatedly. I reached across and held Christine's hand. She withdrew it and placed it back on her lap.

The artist woman chattered on. I saw the coroner glance at his watch. I knew I was next.

"Will it please your honor to call Dr. Simon Hennessey?"

Celia's friend was leaving the witness box. I sidled out from the pew and walked toward it. I kept my eyes on the floor but I could feel the audience-like furnace on the right side of my face. I steadied myself in the witness box and the policeman offered me a Bible.

"Do you swear to tell the truth, the whole truth and nothing but the truth?"

"I do." The words were barely audible. I cleared my throat. "I do," I said again.

The coroner screwed the top on his pen and gave me his full attention. From this vantage point I could see the thick sheaf of papers in front of him—pathologist's reports, medical notes, certificates, statements. . . . Hennessey's CV was probably in there somewhere—an identity in two sheets of paper—the flimsiest possible disguise.

"You are Simon Hennessey, aged twenty-seven, a casualty officer at the Royal Clifton Hospital?"

"That's correct," I said, perjuring myself in my first breath. I tried to look at the audience without focusing on anyone's face and eventually fixed on the leaded glass of the door at the rear of the chamber. I was shaking so much that the front panel of the witness box was rattling softly. The audience couldn't hear this but the coroner obviously could because he said, "Dr. Hennessey, I don't imagine that you will have been in a coroner's court before so I will explain that our function this morning is not to apportion blame. I am more interested in discovering the cause of the tragedy so that a similar thing will not happen in future, hmm?"

I nodded.

"Good," he said. "Good . . . so in your own time perhaps you'll tell us what happened on the evening of the first of May."

I paused a moment to collect my thoughts. "Mrs. Mountford came to the department about eleven o'clock," I began.

"Eleven-fourteen."

". . . yes. I was sitting in the doctors' room so I examined her there."

"And what did she tell you?"

"She told me she'd fallen on her doorstep. She'd tripped on the carpet. Her arm was in a sling."

"Which arm?"

"Her left arm."

"Her right arm," he corrected me, glancing at his notes.

"Sorry—her right arm."

"Go on," he said quickly. I wondered why he'd asked me to start at the beginning when he already knew these facts in some detail. Maybe he wanted to demonstrate that he'd done the groundwork—that, despite the lack of witnesses, he had ways of testing the truth of my story. "Go on," he repeated.

"I examined her arm and noticed that, clinically, she had sustained a Colles' fracture. That's a common fracture of the arm near the wrist. I sent her for an X ray which confirmed this."

"And what were you doing while Mrs. Mountford was having her X ray?"

The question took me unawares and I floundered. "I don't know," I said.

"Did you write your findings on the casualty card?"

"No."

"Why not?"

"I don't know," I said again.

"Well, maybe you were doing something else."

"Oh, yes, I was getting things ready in the plaster room."

"That's the nurse's job, isn't it?"

"Yes." I glanced across to Christine who was looking at me without concern. "We tend to help each other out," I said.

"So where was she at the time?"

I looked at Christine again. She was wearing a dark suit and a white blouse. I was reminded of my first impression of her—the religious frankness of her face. I hesitated.

"Well," Mr. Lovejoy prompted. "Was she in the department?"

"Yes . . . I think so . . . I don't know."

"Well, did you look for her?"

"Yes." I said it without premeditation. It was such a short lie it was out before I could stop it. Of course I had thought it many times in the preceding weeks—not only the lie, but the questions that would follow it—as a chess player must subconsciously follow the consequences of moving a pawn. I had begun to see it not as a lie but as a simplification of the truth. Who can choose reality when it is so messy and demeaning? In front of all these people I couldn't possibly explain the shabby pride that made me rush Celia Mountford into the plaster room, deliberately avoiding Christine—a man like that might be guilty of negligence—might be guilty of impersonation, and the sum of these was murder.

The coroner continued, "Where did you look for her?"

"I don't know—the cubicles, the dressing room."

"And she wasn't in the department?"

"I don't know."

Mr. Lovejoy grimaced impatiently. "Now, I know this department. It is not a big place. If you were seriously looking for Nurse Taylor and she was in the department, then you would have found her—is this not the case?"

"Yes," I said.

"And you did not find her?"

"No."

"So she was not there?" I shot a glance in Christine's direction and found to my surprise that her expression hadn't changed—no anger, no confusion. She'd had the same unnerving composure since she came back from London and I couldn't fathom it.

Mr. Lovejoy said, "I will repeat—it is not our business to apportion blame. We are here simply to discover as accurately as possible what happened, and how it happened, and how to prevent it from happening again."

I nodded, wondering if Lovejoy's briskness was indeed a function of impatience rather than guile. He seemed to be suggesting that the fine details of the truth were immaterial. We were here to document a death—to tidy it up and file it away, to do it quickly and neatly with the minimum of fuss. I looked away from him and saw the policeman who had sworn me in apparently reading a passage from the Bible.

". . . so please," Mr. Lovejoy continued, "speak only for yourself and Nurse Taylor will speak only for herself. We have established that the patient arrived, that you looked for the nurse, failed to find her, and continued on your own. Mrs. Mountford returns from X-ray. Proceed."

"I put the cuff on her arm," I began.

"Is it not customary to ask the patient a few questions first?"

"Yes . . . yes, of course," I stammered. "I asked her if she'd had any operations or serious medical illnesses in the past."

"And her answers?"

"Nothing."

"She said nothing?"

"She said there were none."

"She didn't mention this"—the coroner consulted his notes—"this heart complaint?"

"No."

"But you did ask?"

"Of course," I said.

"Go on."

I launched into a description of the Biers' block I'd supposedly performed on Celia Mountford. It was a textbook description learned from a textbook and bearing little relation to the panic-stricken reality of that ghastly evening. When I'd finished, Mr. Lovejoy said, "So this cuff which leaked—you didn't notice it going down?"

"Not until it was too late."

"Surely you would have noticed when it was fully deflated?"

"It didn't need to deflate fully. Once the pressure had fallen to around her blood pressure, then the cuff would have been useless."

"Even though it appeared inflated?"

"That's correct." I'd anticipated that particular line of inquiry and felt pleased with myself for having it sewn up.

"What's the first thing you noticed which drew your attention to the fact that all was not in order?"

"Her arm . . . Mrs. Mountford's arm . . . turned pink. Showing that the blood was getting through."

"So what did you do?"

"I immediately pumped the cuff up again."

"And then?"

"I'm afraid that's the point at which she stopped breathing . . . I checked her pulse and realized that she had arrested."

When I stopped talking I could hear the court recorder's pen racing over the paper. I caught Mountford's face in the audience. The absence of a smile had changed the whole shape of his head. Lovejoy broke the silence.

"So. Disaster. The patient has stopped breathing. What do you do next?"

"I thumped her on the chest."

"And then?"

"Then I checked her airway."

"And then. . . ?"

"And then inflated her lungs with oxygen."

Lovejoy was flicking through the reports in front of him. "You had already tested the oxygen supply and found that it was within reach?"

"I had to move the trolley," I said, remembering the rubber skid marks on the floor.

"And then. . . ?"

"Then I called Christine . . . Nurse Taylor."

"And this time she responded?"

"Yes."

"Tell me, Dr. Hennessey, if you had had some assistance earlier in the procedure, do you think that Mrs. Mountford's death would have been avoided?"

"Yes," I said, realizing as I gave the answer that I was effectively condemning myself. If Christine convinced them that I had deliberately avoided her, then I'd admitted responsibility for Celia's death.

The coroner was jotting down a note. "Very good. You can step down now."

As I came off the podium the deputy sergeant said, "Call Miss Christine Taylor," and Christine rose from the bench. Our paths crossed directly in front of the coroner and in full view of the audience. It was impossible even to exchange a look with her.

I sat down as she was being sworn in. She identified herself in her clear, powerful voice; then Lovejoy said, "Dr. Hennessey has told us that the first time you saw Mrs. Mountford was after her heart had stopped. Is this correct?"

"Yes."

"What I want to establish is why you weren't with Mrs. Mountford in the first place."

"I was hiding," said Christine.

No one in the audience moved but I could sense a quickening among them—a sudden focus of their communal attention.

The coroner frowned and leaned forward. "I beg your pardon?"

"I was hiding," Christine repeated. "We'd had an argument and I was trying to avoid him."

A look of mild exasperation crossed the coroner's face. He knew the answers that were required and this wasn't one of them.

"Dr. Hennessey didn't tell me that."

"He didn't want to embarrass me."

"This is not a question of avoiding embarrassment."

"I know that."

"Where were you hiding?"

"In the canteen. I went to get a coffee."

"Leaving the department unattended?"

"Yes?"

"Is this your normal practice?"

"No," said Christine. "It's expressly forbidden."

"How long were you away for?"

"Fifteen minutes perhaps."

This was nonsense. There was a coffee machine in the X-ray suite. She'd been in the department when Celia first arrived and I'd seen her passing the door ten minutes later. She must have known I'd been concealing things, yet she'd consciously chosen to shoulder the blame.

Lovejoy, the coroner, was shuffling his notes again. "I have to tell you," he said, "that this is the first time this information has been presented to me. Why have you withheld it until now?"

"I've been out of town."

"Will you step down for a moment."

Christine walked back toward me. When she sat back on the bench I whispered, "You didn't need to say that," but she made no reply.

Meanwhile Thorn had taken the witness box.

"You are Charles Thorn of Leigh Road, Bristol?"

"That is correct."

"You have overall responsibility for the Casualty Department?"

"I do."

"When did you first hear of Mrs. Mountford's death?"

"I was rung by Nurse Taylor at two in the morning."

"By which time there was nothing you could do?"

"I came to the department but . . . no . . . that's correct."

"Nurse Taylor has worked for your department for how long?"

"Two years."

"And during that time you have found her to be a reliable employee?"

"Her record is excellent."

"And Dr. Hennessey?"

Thorn looked across at me. "His work has been satisfactory," he said. His sepulchral tone of voice almost seemed to negate this but the coroner seemed uninterested in such subtleties.

"So in your estimation, Dr. Thorn, what was the cause of this accident?"

Thorn seemed to be struggling with some inner conflict, but what he said was, "I wasn't there so I can't say. It's departmental policy that there should be two people in attendance for such procedures and, for whatever reasons, that wasn't adhered to. I suppose the unforeseen element was the failure of the equipment."

They called the resident after that and he gave an account of the resuscitation attempt, then the pathologist who described the postmortem changes. For the benefit of the court he was obliged to phrase this in nontechnical terms. He said he hadn't found much alcohol in Celia Mountford's bloodstream. She hadn't had a conventional heart attack but due to the poison in her system the heart had stopped beating and the tissues of her brain had died as a result.

The last witness was the maintenance engineer who'd looked at the blood-pressure cuff. He said there was a small leak but he didn't know how it had been caused. The equipment hadn't been serviced for a few months.

Throughout the proceedings I'd watched Mountford dwindle in stature. With this final piece of evidence his face began to contort. He left the court before the summing up.

Lovejoy leaned back in his chair and cracked his knuckles again. The clock above his head said twelve-thirty. It had taken less than two hours to wrap the whole thing up. He squared the papers in front of him and checked his watch. He looked pleased that everything had gone so smoothly.

Lovejoy was saying, ". . . The patient died as a result of an anesthetic which was performed properly but without assistance. Nurse Taylor has told us how she blames herself for this but I'm sure her impeccable record of service will be taken into account. Dr. Hennessey, you must realize that things might have gone differently if you had waited for the nurse and if you had checked the anesthetic equipment before commencing. Apart from that, the accident must be attributed to an unforeseen failure of equipment. Such is the price we unfortunately pay for the complexity of modern medical treatment. The verdict here, as in similar cases, must surely be 'Death by Misadventure.'"

It was a neat, compact summary and he delivered it with obvious satisfaction. In the courtroom there was a general easing of muscles and straightening of cramped limbs. I was reminded of the end of my father's funeral— the same undertow of relief. Obligations had been discharged and duty seen to be done.

The policeman got us all to stand up again while the coroner left; then we duly filed out, blinking, into the lobby. A couple of people I didn't recognize shook my hand. Thorn left without speaking to anyone. Mountford was nowhere to be seen.

I told Christine I'd drive her back to her flat and she followed me out into the sunshine.

CHAPTER
29

I'D PARKED ON UPPER MAUDLIN STREET, outside the University Drama Department. There wasn't a cloud in the sky—it felt like the first day of summer. I let the car roof down, then took off my jacket and tie and threw them in the backseat.

"Thank God that's over with."

"Yes," she said.

I leaned over to kiss her and she offered me her cheek. I started up the engine and we pulled away. "I really appreciate what you did."

"What did I do?"

"Taking the blame like that."

"That's all right," she said. "I had nothing to lose."

The lights at the top of Park Street were red. I stopped opposite the Wills building.

"What do you mean, nothing to lose?"

"I've resigned."

"You're not serious?"

"Of course I am."

"Why, for God's sake?"

"You know why."

"I don't know why. When did you decide this?"

"Last week."

"Why didn't you tell me?"

She shrugged. "I was in London."

Behind me a horn tooted and I noticed the traffic was moving. We lurched off, stopped again opposite the city art gallery.

"I thought you enjoyed nursing."

"I used to." She was holding the hair out of her face with one hand.

"So what's changed?"

"I don't know," she said. "Maybe I have. It was quite true, that stuff you said the night it happened, about my bogus piety. Underneath I was just the same as you—worrying about *me*. Not about Celia Mountford. I guess it takes a tragedy like that to reveal to you the extent of your own selfishness. It happened once a long time ago when we were playing for the first time at the ICA and the Sparks, whom we'd known for two years, was electrocuted and killed, and my first thought was, 'Damn, they'll have to close the show. There goes our big break.' I thought I'd changed since then but I haven't. This wonderful caring person I'd become was just a front."

"You're being ridiculous," I said. "You're the most selfless person I know."

"There are different kinds of selfishness."

"You look after people, you work bloody long hours. I've seen you with those horrible old men and women, patting their heads, undressing them. You worry about the health of complete strangers—if that's not selflessness I don't know what is."

"I do it because it makes me feel good. It's an image I have of myself."

"Christine, I don't know why we're having this conversation. It doesn't bother me if you don't think you're a good person. I just think it's a stupid idea for giving up nursing. You're bloody good at the job. You make a lot of people happy. You seem to enjoy it . . ."

"I don't enjoy it."

"Why are you being like this? You're standing everything on its head. You're happy at your work. I know you are."

"It's a trick—I'm very good at it."

"For Christ's sake, I've lived with you for four months."

"My parents lived together for twenty-four years and the one never knew what the other was thinking. It's like being in a long-running soap opera—after a while the roles become indistinguishable from real life."

I drove on in silence past the statue of George IV and the incongruous shop, wedged in a corner beyond it, which advertised "All Pet Needs." I'd been feeling euphoric after the trial but now she'd managed to infuriate me by denying what I knew to be the truth. I was reminded of Mountford becoming belligerent at the dinner table. There is nothing more exasperating than someone tampering with reality.

"So what are you planning to do?" I said huffily.

"Go back to acting."

I shook my head. "Where?"

"London."

"When were you planning to go?"

"This evening. Before people start pestering me to stay."

"What about me? I don't suppose you'll miss me."

"Come on, Simon. You know it's over."

"What do you mean, 'It's over'? We just got out of this mess. You don't have to resign. You don't have to leave. Everything was fine the way it was."

"We'd be living a lie. We know too much about each other."

"What do you mean? You've gone mad. You're talking nonsense."

She turned toward me, still holding her hair back and shouted above the noise of the engine, "Listen to me, Simon, I'm serious. You can't deny the past. That stuff with Celia happened and we both know how we reacted. We've seen through each other. Love can't survive that."

"It's all behind us," I said, turning into the Paragon. "Now we go back to normal."

"Normal is different now, Simon. That was part of 'Normal.'"

She got out of the car and slammed the door.

"Can I come up?" I asked.

"If you like."

She'd obviously spent the previous night clearing up the flat. There were four big plastic rubbish bags just inside the door and all the trinkets had been cleared from the top of her bookshelves. I sat numbly on the edge of the bed while she finished emptying the cupboards, packing some items, discarding the rest.

"What about your books?"

"I'll leave them. Someone else can read them."

"Well, the furniture then?"

"It came with the flat."

"What about the cat?" I asked.

"I'm taking her with me."

"Where can I reach you?"

"You can't reach me. I don't want you to try."

"You know. Don't you?"

"Know what?" She stopped halfway across the bedroom with a mohair cardigan in one hand and two pairs of shoes in the other.

"Nothing," I said. "Do you want to grab a meal at Carey's?"

"No. There's a train at eight-thirty—I'll catch it if I hurry."

"This is insane. You're being insane."

She continued folding clothes and packing them in her suitcase. I went through to the lounge and put on a record.

"I'll run you to the station then," I said.

"You don't have to. I've booked a taxi."

"What about the rest of this stuff?"

"Keep it. Sell it. Chuck it out. It doesn't mean anything to me anymore."

She got the cat into the traveling basket just as the bell rang and I helped her downstairs to the waiting Ford Granada and the driver loaded her stuff into the boot.

I stood at the end of the crescent watching long after the car had disappeared, then I turned and walked back up the green-lit stairwell. Inside, the main room of her flat looked bigger and emptier than ever before. I wandered through to her bedroom and looked across the Gorge to the hospital. I still had my job there and my false identity had survived the crisis but it now felt like rather a pyrrhic victory. I ran myself a deep bath and sat in it morbidly enumerating the people who disliked or mistrusted me—Christine, Molly, Thorn, Mountford. . . . Christine had been right; time goes on and we only accumulate mistakes.

I worked the next morning and spent the afternoon clearing out my room. Molly came in as I was packing my suitcase.

"Where you off to then?"

"I'm moving into a flat."

"What flat?"

"Just a flat," I said, kneeling on the lid to make it close.

"Be with that nurse, don't it?" she said, reaching up to straighten the calender. "I thought she'd left."

"It's not with the nurse," I told her, standing up. I

could see no reason for telling her where I was moving to and I got a certain satisfaction from frustrating her inquiries.

"She still in town then?"

"I'm rather busy, Molly."

She gave a little "harrumph" and stumped off down the stairs to get on with her cleaning. I took my suitcase down to the car and went back for the jackets and coats. I was loading these on to the backseat when I met Adam in tennis whites, coming out of the residence.

"You moving out?" he asked.

"Yeah, Christine's gone back to London so she's given me her flat."

"Need a hand with anything?"

"No, it's kind of you."

"Can you give me a lift over the bridge then?"

"Sure, jump in."

As we drove across the bridge Adam said, "I hear you put up a pretty good show at the inquest."

"I just told them what happened," I said.

"Sure, but, you know, it's a reflection on all of us. Here, let me get this." Adam handed me twenty pence for the toll booth. The barrier lifted.

"I rather felt I'd let everyone down," I said.

"Not a bit of it. We've all had narrow scrapes. I bet there's not a doctor in this hospital who doesn't feel responsible for someone's death. You just drew the short straw. It's an occupational hazard, the public should realize that. Otherwise we end up with a situation like America. Gosh, those poor buggers."

We laughed heartily and I drove him to the Clifton Tennis Club. He invited me in for a drink.

Over the next few days it dawned on me that, rather than discrediting me in the eyes of my peers the accident had turned me into something of a folk hero. I'd touched a

common nerve. I remembered the warm handshakes immediately after the inquest and the messages of support
before it. Now I kept getting accosted by relative strangers who said, as Adam had, that they had every confidence in me and it could have happened to anybody.

In the following week I began to capitalize on this. I
had always shied clear of my contemporaries for fear of
having to talk about my past but now, with the inquest
fresh in everyone's memory, I had a ready-made topic for
conversation. I began to socialize more in the doctors'
mess and to make myself more amenable to company. On
more than one occasion I found myself at the center of a
group comprising Adam, Hillary, Tony, Kassim and the
others, holding forth on the trial and the events that preceded it.

The same closing of ranks probably explained why
Thorn, at the inquest, hadn't expressed any doubts about
my competence. It struck me now that there had been a
greater issue at stake—the public image of the hospital.
To denounce me at the trial was to denounce his very
profession, and whatever his personal morality, Thorn
was too dyed in the wool to contemplate that.

Emboldened by this new feeling of fraternity I
stopped trying to avoid him. The next time we passed in
the corridor I greeted him with a cheerful "hello."

This was four days after the trial, but he was still
wearing a black tie and seemed untypically vacant.

He stopped and peered into my face as though trying to recognize me and then said, "Yes, what is it?"

I hadn't intended to engage him in conversation but
having brought him to a halt I felt that something was
required of me.

"I haven't had the chance to tell you," I said, "how
much I appreciated your support at the inquest."

"Support?" he said.

"I'm terribly sorry for any embarrassment I may
have caused you."

"You're sorry. Hmph . . . I can't tell you, Hennessey, you won't know . . . how much . . . these few moments of carelessness have cost . . . to all of us."

"I've written a letter to Dr. Mountford," I said.

Thorn studied his hands. "I'm afraid he won't read it."

"I didn't realize he felt that bitter."

"He doesn't feel bitter," said Thorn softly. "He doesn't feel anything. He killed himself at home on Sunday."

The news horrified me but later this was tempered with relief. It would have been damned embarrassing to see Mountford in the hospital again and I hadn't been looking forward to his return to work.

I looked at the floor. "I didn't know," I said.

"Obviously not."

Then Thorn seemed to collect himself and carried on toward the stairway.

I learned afterward that Mountford had blown the back of his head off with both barrels of his Purdy shotgun. I remember him telling me about the small estate in Perthshire.

His cleaning lady had found the body propped up in his study. The rows of old medical books behind him had absorbed the noise, the spent shot, and most of the blood. Even in death he was a very tidy man.

CHAPTER 30

Dear Dr. Hennessey,

Thank you for your application for the post of SHO in General Surgery. We acknowledge that, due to the tragic death of your previous employer, Dr. Mountford, no reference will be available. His secretary has, however, forwarded copies of your previous references which seem quite satisfactory.

I would like to see you for an interview in about three weeks' time. Please contact my department to arrange a suitable date.

Yours sincerely,
Mr. Henry Evans MBChB FRCS
Consultant Surgeon
Salisbury General Hospital

CHAPTER
31

THE INTERVIEW AT SALISBURY CAME IN the first weeks of July and there was never much doubt that I'd get the job. I can't remember a period of my life when I felt more charmed. The summer days and nights seemed to last forever. Tennis at the club with Adam or swimming with Andrea at the university pool.

Once we drove up the Wye valley and off the road and across the fields. We felled a tree and rolled it down the slope to the river where we could sit on it and paddle ourselves through the slow, warm water. We lay on our backs in the grass till the sun set and made jokes about cases we'd seen or patients we'd treated. It seemed to me we were the chosen race, the elite, the masters of life and death, loafing in Parnassus.

One night a group of us drove to Clevedon where

the old broken pier is falling into the sea; we lay on the sand behind a bonfire and drank beer and listened to cassettes. I remember the evening because Hillary stood on a rusting spike and slit the heel of one foot. Later, back in the Casualty Department, I flushed it with peroxide and sewed it up for her.

One of the ENT surgeons called Nigel Enfield invited us all up to a weekend party in his parents' house—an old watermill on the Vale of Evesham. We barbecued sausages and rowed up the river. I'd bought myself a camera by then and had begun to compile an album like Simon Hennessey's. Our lives had now merged so completely that it would have been difficult to see where his ended and mine began—the same scenes of untroubled privilege, the same euphoric, open faces, the same trappings of luxury. I had made it.

For the most part, it amazed me how quickly and how completely I had managed to forget Christine. Occasionally, at the end of an evening, when the couples began to pair off, I would experience the odd rather pleasurable pang of loneliness, but as for missing her—no, I can't say I did. Maybe she was right when she said that our affair had ended some time before. What I did miss was the sex but I'd been making some progress in that direction with Andrea Leighton, the Medical House Officer. She had a rather aristocratic accent and nicely rounded breasts. On odd mornings off work we'd go swimming in the university pool—ostensibly as part of a fitness drive. With each successive visit we spent less and less time swimming and more time fooling about at the shallow end. I'd reached the stage when physical contact was acceptable—like holding her feet when she swam with her arms. In fact we were in this position when the bomb dropped.

I'd caught only a glimpse of the green and purple shorts as he dived in at the deep end, I couldn't remember who wore them but I knew instinctively that he was someone I wanted to avoid.

He swam a long way underwater and was almost a third of the way down the pool before he surfaced. He swam another couple of strokes with his head down but by then I was certain—that fuzzy red hair—it could only be one person.

I let go of Andrea's legs and was out of the pool like a shot. She floundered and called out to me as I headed for the men's changing room. I turned briefly to signal that I'd be back in a moment and at that instant Alec's head popped out of the water. He stopped swimming and raised the goggles onto his forehead.

As I reached the changing-room door I heard him call the word I had hoped never to hear again.

"Matthew!"

It reverberated around the changing room like an alarm bell. I darted for my locker and tried to lever the key out of the rubber band at my wrist. It fell on the floor. When I tried to pick it up it was stuck to the wet damp tiles. I prised it off and fumbled with the lock. I flung open the door, and seized an armful of clothes— shirt, trousers, jacket and shoes. One of my socks fell in some water as I rushed for the cubicles. At that instant the changing-room door opened, I dived into the nearest booth. There was no lock on the door.

"Matthew?"

I could hear Alec padding along the rows, calling my name and opening doors. I heard him apologize to someone who was changing in one of the other booths.

"Matthew?" he called again.

I was trying to pull a shirt on but it was sticking to my wet skin. I didn't have a hope of avoiding him. When he opened the door of my cubicle I was stuck with my head wrapped in cotton, trying to get my fist through the armholes. The disguise didn't fool him.

"Matthew!"

I emerged from the shirt looking sheepish. Alec was slightly thinner but otherwise just as I remembered him. I stood, half naked, my sinuses full of water, blinking from the chlorine.

"Hello, Alec."

"What are you doing here?"

"Swimming."

He laughed at this and punched me lightly in the stomach.

"Same old Matthew," he said "You haven't changed a bit. Didn't you hear me calling?"

I shook my head. "Water in the ears."

"I thought you were trying to avoid me."

"No, it's great to see you."

"Well, how's things?"

I'd forgotten how loud his voice was I scrubbed my hair with my towel. I've never felt more utterly exposed. At any moment someone I knew might come into the changing rooms and find us together.

"Fine, just fine."

"Are you living nearby?"

"Let me get dressed," I told him. "I don't have a lot of time to talk right now."

"That's OK. We could meet later "

"How long are you in Bristol?"

"I'm here to stay," he said.

It was perfectly warm in the changing room but I found myself shivering.

"You've got a job here?"

"I will have."

"Whereabouts?"

"The Royal Clifton Hospital."

A sense of unreality enveloped me.

"Starting when?" I heard myself ask.

"Next week. I'm here to find somewhere to stay."

I sat down, feeling weak. "What's the job?"

"Nursing. Didn't you get my letter?"

"What letter? How did you know where I was?"

"I didn't. I sent it to the Turks and Caicos. Did you have a good time there?"

"Yes. Brilliant. Get your clothes."

"I thought you were rushing off."

"This is more important."

"What's the problem?"

"No problem. Let's get out of here."

"Where are we going?"

"I know a place in the country," I said. "I'll take you for a drink."

"Now you're talking."

We dressed together as we had dressed on numerous occasions at the West Harwood Hospital with Alec calling jokes to me over the partition. They were the same old jokes but right now I found none of them funny. I pulled on my underpants and trousers, hunted for my socks and crammed my feet viciously into my shoes. With every second I could feel my resentment growing. Why here of all places? Why did he have to come here? Why now? Just when I had succeeded in reinventing myself. I winced every time he called me Matthew. Matthew Harris was dead. It had taken me five bloody, nerveracking months to kill him and now this blundering Celtic oaf was digging up the grave. Alec used almost to be a friend but I have never hated anyone so completely, so passionately, as I hated him then.

CHAPTER
32

I STOOD OUTSIDE ALEC'S CUBICLE AS he finished putting on his trousers. "Get a move on."

"Hold your horses."

He tied his laces and we left.

I got him into the car and drove off before anyone could see us. We drove out of town round the back of the university, through Montpelier.

"So you had fun on the yachting trip?" he asked as we turned on to the M32.

"Sure, it was great."

"You don't have much of a suntan."

"It's worn off in the last couple of months."

"So what have you been doing in Britain?"

"This and that." I shouted above the noise of the engine.

"Back to portering?"

I nodded equivocally.

"Ha-ha. Thought you were giving that up for good, eh? Oh, well, back to the grindstone. Where are you working? Not Bristol?"

"No," I said. "No, no." The tires protested as I whirled under the M4 and headed up the eastbound ramp.

"Where then?"

"Salisbury."

"Is that near here?"

"Near enough."

"Nice?"

"Yes."

"Well," he said, "it's a small world."

I nodded bitterly in agreement. Too bloody small. We hit sixty. The wheels of the car were out of alignment and it vibrated like crazy at this speed. I accelerated out of it but even after the car had settled down my hands continued to vibrate on the steering wheel.

We took the Bath turnoff, then headed north along country lanes into the burgeoning wilderness.

Coombe is a collection of Cotswold-stone houses lost in time. I'd discovered it with Christine two months previously. Now, drenched in foliage, it seemed even more medieval and mysterious than before. The sun was already dropping when we arrived, throwing blades of shadow across the hillside. I parked near the top and we walked down into the shrouded valley.

Emerging in the village we turned past the market cross and along between the rows of cottages. The day's heat was still radiating from the cobbles as we made our way to the turreted hotel at the heart of the valley.

The hotel was set in its own grounds—acres of lawn and trees as dense as haystacks. I left Alec on the bench next to the millpond while I went inside to get some beers. There was no one in the lounge and it took some time for a girl to arrive at the bar. I bought two pints of Tetley's. When I returned Alec was throwing sticks into the sluice from the dam. I checked my watch. I was on duty back at the hospital in three hours' time.

We sat on the bench and drank. A cluster of mayflies were hovering above the pond, just out of reach of the jumping fish.

"Tell me about your job," I said. "Have you definitely accepted it?"

"Oh, aye, it's in the bag."

"What does it involve?"

"It's a rotation—you know—move round all the departments, two months here, three months there. Exams twice a year, answer all the questions and win a gong."

He smiled at this. I didn't.

"You wouldn't think of chucking it in?" I asked.

"Do what?" Alec said. "I've not even started."

"That's what I mean. Don't start. Do something else."

Alec scowled. "You may think nursing's a shit job but I'm happy with it."

"How's the money?" I asked.

"I don't know. Six or seven grand."

"Not very much, is it?"

"The money's not important."

"Listen," I said, "suppose I give you a thousand pounds not to work here." It was a crass, clumsy ploy but I was desperate.

Alec just laughed.

"I'm serious."

"Sure, of course you are."

"Well, what would you say?"

He looked at me, still smiling with half of his mouth. "Well, I'd refuse."

"What's so special about Bristol?"

"Come on, Matthew, you've had your joke. What is this?"

I said, "Why Bristol? Why did you have to come here?"

"I like it. It's a nice place. . . . Look at it—lots of countryside . . . plus you're here?"

"That's just the point," I said. "I'm here."

He looked at me for a long time, then his face hardened. "You're telling me you don't want me around, is that it?"

"Yes, that's it."

"Fair enough, pal, it's a big place."

"I'm working at the Royal Clifton," I told him.

"You said you were working in Salisbury."

"Well, I'm not—not for another month."

"You're an orderly at the Royal Clifton?"

"No."

"Make your mind up."

"I'm not working as an orderly," I said, exasperated beyond caution. "I'm working as a doctor."

An uncertain smile flickered across Alex's face.

"Come again?"

"You remember Simon Hennessey—the doc who was killed? I stole his papers and applied for his job here. I'm working as a doctor."

"Instead?"

"Yes."

A fish rose out of the water, snatched at a fly, and plopped back into the pond.

"Just like that?"

"Just like that," I said.

"So how did you. . . ?"

"I learned it. Remember that game we used to play?"

"Come on, man, that was guessing. What is it? Five, six months? You can't possibly have had enough time."

"I had all the time I needed."

Alec shook his head. "You can't do it."

"I am doing it, Alec. I've been doing it since I got here. They all think I'm a doctor."

I didn't know how I'd expected him to react to all this—laughter, incredulity perhaps. But not this, not this stony horror. He was making me nervous and the beer I was holding was beginning to slop over the sides of the glass. I put it down. I had the dreadful feeling that I'd got myself in too deep but now I couldn't go back. Alec was now staring woodenly at the pond.

"So you see how it is," I said. "It's best for me if you don't work here at all. If you do, then you'll have to pretend not to know me."

I looked across at him. The evening light was turning red and his hair looked as though it was on fire.

"I don't know."

"What don't you know?"

"I don't know," he said more loudly. "You can't just go around impersonating people. Not doctors. You don't know enough. You're lethal."

"They're all lethal. It's a dangerous job. I'm no worse than the rest of them."

"You're telling me you've killed someone."

"Of course not, it's been a piece of cake."

Alec contemplated the grass at length, biting his lip.

"OK?" I asked.

"No, it's not OK," he said. "I'll need to think about it."

"I don't want you to think about it," I shouted. "I'm asking for a month's silence. Then I'll be off. Three weeks. OK? I want you to agree now. Before we go back into town, before you start your job, that you won't try to contact me. All right? That's all I want you to do. It's nothing."

"It's not nothing. What is it with you, Matthew? You're mad. You're asking me to take part in a crime."

"I'm asking you nothing of the sort, Alec. I'm just asking you to keep your mouth shut."

"It's the same thing."

"It's not the same thing."

"Something could go wrong. What then?"

I said, "That's my probem, OK? Just let me deal with it. You've got nothing to worry about."

"Oh, sure. Except that when you go down I go with you."

"Well, get out then. Leave," I said. "You never met me. I'm asking you to go."

Alec shook his head. "It's too late," he said. "I know now—you can't change that."

"You can't change the past."—It was so close to Christine's parting words that it briefly took the wind out of my sails.

"I've done no one any harm," I said.

"That's not the point." Alec was all puffed up now, standing up, walking precariously close to the edge of the millrace. "You can't just choose to be someone you're not. You can't deceive people like that. Doctors train for six years!"

"You think that makes any difference?" I asked him. "You think those six years matter to the patients? What do they do for six years—heat up test tubes? Look at anatomy charts? You've seen students on the wards. You know most of them are still incompetent. I'm as good as any of those bastards."

"You're a theater orderly," said Alec.

"I'm not a theater orderly, you dickhead. I happen to have worked as a theater orderly. Now I'm working as a doctor and making a bloody good job of it."

"You're a charlatan," he said.

"The word's out of date. The whole idea's out of date. The man who fixes your fridge is a charlatan. The man who mends your car is a charlatan. We're all pretending to be more competent than we actually are. That's how people get on in the world. If you do a half-decent job no one gives a damn."

Alec sat down and got up again. "Mechanics, OK,"

he said, "but a doctor. A doctor, for Christ's sake!"

"It's just a job," I told him. "And a simple, repetitive job at that. You just think it's complex because they want you to believe it's complex. You said that once yourself. And it's true. You ask anyone—and I don't care what they work as—you ask them if someone half intelligent can learn to do their job in two months and I guarantee they'll say yes."

"But . . . but . . ."

"But what?"

"But you don't have any qualifications," said Alec.

"To hell with them. That's what I'm saying. To hell with them. They're a con. It's only morons like you who believe they mean anything."

I stopped, panting. Alec walked away and turned his back on me.

"I don't agree with you," he said.

"Of course you don't. Why else should you be signing on for three years' training which allows you, what, to pour other people's shit down the sluice?"

He said, "At least it's honest."

"Fuck you, Alec." I drained my glass and chucked it at the far side of the millpond. It hit the rocks and shattered. I turned and strode off across the deserted lawn in the direction of the car. I knew I couldn't leave Alec. I knew I had to try to persuade him before we got back to Bristol but just then I was too annoyed to talk.

With the disappearance of the sun, the sky had turned a cold, deep blue. I walked faster, up the hill, my mind and body both working in top gear. Alec of all people. He could ruin everything. I got to the car, put the hood up and sat inside, stewing, and looked to see if he was following. No sign of him. I looked at my watch—half past eight. I was due in at work at ten. I had ninety minutes to persuade him to leave Bristol and he already seemed intractable. The chances of my succeeding were zero. Where the hell was he? I imagined him puffing up the hill—everything had been rosy before he arrived. I'd got a new job to look forward to. The Celia Mountford affair was behind me . . . just.

Alec had asked if I'd killed anyone. If he worked in the Royal Clifton he'd learn about Celia. If he learned about Celia he'd turn me in. If he turned me in I was finished.

Medicine is the only profession that sanctions murder. As Simon Hennessey I could be forgiven even for the death of my boss's wife. But as Matthew Harris I could be put away for life. For all my cant about the uselessness of paper qualifications, they provided the flimsy barrier between me and the Old Bailey. The stakes in my game of impersonation had become agonizingly high and now Alec was weighting the dice against me.

I started up the engine. It was going to be an accident, everything happens by accident. I got the job by accident. Celia's death had been an accident. God knows I didn't want her to die. Neither did I want Alec to die but circumstances had conspired against him. It was in the hands of the gods. Maybe he'd jump out of the way in time. I hoped he would, I hoped he wouldn't. I sat, a hapless passenger as the car careered round one corner, then the next. The road was a spiraling green tunnel. I rounded the third corner and there he was, legs apart, dazzled like a rabbit in the glare of the headlights. Did I put my foot on the accelerator or did the steering wheel wrench out of my hands? I really can't remember. I have chosen to forget, but, at odd moments, fragments of the following sequence still pop into my consciousness as though searching for the other components in that defect in my memory. I remember the noise of the engine revving, the sweep of the headlights, Alec's shocked face frozen halfway between fear and amazement. The front wheels rearing over his body. Then silence.

I switched off the engine and peered in the rearview mirror for signs of movement—nothing. I drove down the hill, did a three-point turn and came back. His body was lying where I'd hit it at the side of the road. It was dark under the trees and the angle of the car on the hill made it difficult to throw much light on him. I got out, spastic with anticipation, and walked toward him. He didn't move. I reached down and gingerly lifted an arm. It was warm but limp. I put a hand on one side of his neck next to the windpipe. I could feel no pulse.

Dead.

I rifled through his pockets and found his wallet. Somehow, in removing it, I got a lot of blood on my fingers. I wiped my sticky hand on a piece of grass and hurried back to the car, then got in and drove.

CHAPTER
33

THEY SAY YOU CAN GROW ACCUSTOMED to murder but I doubt it. I got back in the car, almost weeping when the engine stalled, then grinding the gears as I hurled it up the hill. I drove back to the motorway like a maniac, careering through the corners, branches tearing at the roof and at the sides of the car. Potholes seemed to leap out of the road and slam against the chassis. I could hardly believe my own stupidity—there were so many ways of getting caught now; anyone might have seen the car parked at the top of the hill; anyone might have seen Alec and me together.

I gunned back down the M4 and swerved out into the fast lane, foot hard on the floor, my arms braced against the wheel. It had taken twenty minutes to get out to Coombe but I drove back in ten. By the time I hit Clifton I'd just about extinguished the raging death wish.

I drove round the back of the department and parked behind the boiler house. There was a dent in the hood of the car with a long splash of blood reaching almost to the windshield. I went into the department, shaky as a colt, and soaked some paper towels in hot water, then went back out and tried to wipe the blood off. Some of it had dried and my efforts merely produced a pale halo which made it even more conspicuous. I gave up and went back in.

In the on-call room I got myself cleaned up, put on a white coat and came out ready for action. As I worked I was haunted by the idea that Alec might revive. I knew this was just a trick of my conscience. He was dead all right. I'd hit him doing forty and his head had come down hard on the hood. I cursed my own squeamishness—if I hadn't been so windy I'd have been able to make sure that he was finished.

Time passed and the familiar world of minor domestic accident closed around me. A kid came in who'd caught his finger in a folding chair and I spent half an hour sewing the tip back on. A drunk came with a gashed elbow and I sewed that up too. A bedraggled young attempted suicide came in. It was just Mogadon she'd taken so I sent her on to the on-call medic for observation overnight. We had another student who'd overdosed on magic mushrooms and was hallucinating wildly. The new nurse, Jenny, pumped his stomach. It was a night like any other—a carload of legal secretaries who'd hit a post, an old lady who'd fallen off her commode and fractured her hip, a child who'd swallowed a marble, a gas fitter on night shift with a speck of copper filing in his eye. I lost myself in the work and the image of Alec staggering along some Cotswold lane faded into the realm of nightmare. By twelve-thirty I was ready for bed.

I changed into my theater pajamas and got under the covers. They made me too hot so I threw everything off. I'd no sooner closed my eyes than the nurse called

Jenny opened the door. I squinted to see her against the dazzling light from the department.

"Phone for you," she said.

I swung my legs out of bed and put my clogs on.

The red receiver for Ambulance Control was lying on the table in the doctors' room. Jenny was speaking on the other phone.

"This is Dr. Hennessey."

"Hello, doc." The night controller had just started work and his voice was unsettlingly loud. "We've got a bad RTA coming in—just so you're ready."

I borrowed Jenny's pen to write on the back of an X-ray request form.

"What's he got?"

"Full house. Head injury, ribs, possible spleen, possible pelvis. Femur on one side, tib and fib on the other."

"Christ, what happened to him?"

"Hit and run near Coombe . . . hello, hello . . . You still there, doc? . . . Hello?"

"Yes," I said, "I'm still here. Why are you bringing him to us?"

"The Royal Clifton's on take."

"Frenchay's nearer," I said. "He sounds bad—take him to Frenchay."

"He's already on his way. He'll be with you in ten minutes."

An arctic current was coursing through my veins. I stood, shivering in my theater pajamas.

"Is he conscious?"

"I can't tell you."

"Radio the ambulance and ask them then."

"No point, doc. They'll be right with you. Bye now."

"Wait," I shouted but the line was already dead.

I put the phone down and stood staring at the desk.

I'd used up what few psychological resources I had long ago. I had nothing left for this final crisis.

"Sounds serious, doesn't it?" Jenny said.

"Very."

I'll look out some Thomas splints and run through the Haemmaccel. Dr. Thorn says he's on the way in."

"He's what?"

"He's coming in. He'll be here in twenty minutes. He said after the Mountford case that we had to inform him of any serious crises." She delivered the last of this over her shoulder as she stepped past me toward the major-accident suite. She found me in the same position a minute later when she came back looking for her pen.

"Did you ring the Orthopods and General Surgery?" she asked.

"No."

"Shall I?"

She reached for the phone. I stepped in front of her. "No," I said, "I'll look after it."

I went to pee and stood in the loo. Somewhere, in the back of an ambulance, Alec, my nemesis, was hurtling toward me. God let him not be conscious. The world had gone crazy. I was locked into an insane poker game which I could no longer afford to stop playing. After killing Celia Mountford, attempting to murder Alec had perhaps been a necessary risk. Now I was forced to finish the job even if it meant doing so directly under Thorn's nose. That Alec had to die was certain—I was already up to my elbows in innocent blood—one death on my hands already, two if you counted her husband's suicide. Making it three hardly seemed to matter.

I rummaged about for the Marcaine. If it worked for Celia it would probably work for Alec. I found a box of vials and started foraging for a 50 mil. syringe. Getting it out of the cellophane package and drawing up the fluid seemed to take forever. My hands were floppy rubber replicas of themselves. I smashed two vials and got glass in the end of my thumb before I managed to draw one up. I swept the detritus into a rubbish bin and pocketed the full syringe just as the ambulance came into earshot. I walked out of the department into the ambulance bay under the ferocious glare of the mercury lights.

CHAPTER
34

THE SIREN DIED WITH A STIFLED yowl. The driver got out. It was a warm evening and he was still in shirt sleeves. I watched as he came round my side of the van and flung open the doors. I hung back. I didn't want to go in there. The ambulance man inside detached a drip bag. As the driver lifted the stretcher and backed past me I glimpsed Alec's face. His skin was deathly white with a tracery of dried blood descending from the forehead.

We burst through the swing doors and into resus. Suddenly there were a million people around—Jenny and a student nurse, the two ambulance men, an orderly and the X-ray technician. I was caught up, despite myself, in the role I had chosen to play—now obliged to revive the one man in the world I most desperately wanted dead.

"One, two, three, lift," said the ambulance men.

I looked into Alec's eyes, inspected the boggy swelling on his skull, checked his throat for blood and vomit, tugged at his teeth and felt for his carotid. Earlier, in my panic, the pulse had eluded me but now, damn it, it was just detectable.

Jenny was already cutting off his clothes with a huge pair of scissors. She exposed his white, hairless chest and I noticed the dimpling of broken ribs every time he took a breath. She cut up both sides of his trousers and peeled them apart to reveal the bruised pelvis. His left thigh was bowed and the lower right leg was broken below the knee. There was a bruise corresponding to the tread of my car tire clearly visible on the surrounding skin. He wasn't the first bad car accident I'd seen but he was undoubtedly the most horrific—I could read on his body the sequence of my assault on him—the smashed thigh and pelvis where the front of the car had struck him, the crushed ribs where he'd doubled over the hood, the battered skull where his head had come down on it, then the crushed right leg that had been dragged under the wheel. I surveyed my handiwork, willing him to die.

Jenny said, "I told you you'd need General and Ortho."

"I'll ring them," I said.

"Better ring Anesthetics too—his breathing's not too hot."

"OK, OK," I shouted. The ambulance men looked up. Jenny clicked her tongue and went to look out some stuff from the wall cupboards. I was aware of the X-ray technician—a fresh-faced lad with a squint—hanging around at my elbow.

"What do you want?" I snapped.

He handed me an X-ray form, I scribbled down *Skull, pelvis, left ribs, chest, cervical spine, right femur, left tib and fib* and handed it back, if only to get rid of him. He went off to get some cassettes. The ambulance men were still waiting to see if they could help. I told them to leave. As they walked out through the swing doors. I saw two thickset policemen in the doctors' room. The doors swung shut. The student nurse wheeled up a drip set.

"Hold his arm," I said.

She handed me a gray Venflon and I threaded it into the vein in Alec's arm. I remembered the first time I'd done this, on Mr. Gough. I'd had more experience since then but now there was a lot more resting on my success. It slipped in smoothly and I hitched up the drip.

"Get me a twenty-mil. syringe. Label blood tubes for full blood count, electrolytes and transfusion."

This was all in Alec's interest but it got the nurse out of the way long enough for me to get the syringe of Marcaine out of my pocket. I was fitting it on to the Venflon in his arm when Jenny came back and started shaving Alec's leg for the Thomas splint.

"Will you ring the surgeons now?" I asked, trying to conceal the syringe under the sheet.

She glared at me and threw the razor on the floor, then stalked over to the phone. I'd forgotten there was a wall phone there—she could still see me clearly from where she stood. I cursed, slipped the syringe back into my pocket and started trying to look busy again. Alec's eyes were still closed, his lips were parted, caked with dark crusts. His saliva was tinged red with blood from his bruised right lung. I stuffed a Guedel's airway into his mouth and put an oxygen mask over it.

Jenny was still talking to the switchboard, trying to get hold of the surgeons. The student nurse came back with the blood bottles I'd requested so I sent her off to get a cervical collar. I felt like the romantic lead in a French farce, trying desperately to be alone in a room with three doors. Jenny turned her back on me, still talking. I was reaching for the syringe of Marcaine again when the kid from X-ray came back.

"Ready to shoot?"

The syringe went back in my pocket.

"OK," I said. "Go ahead." The fact that X rays were in progress would get everybody out of the room. Jenny put the phone down and left. I noticed one of the policemen looking in through the oval window so I pulled one of the screens across. The X-ray technician was asking me to support Alec's body as he slipped the cassettee underneath it. He started lining up on Alec's chest, reaching to maneuver the bulky black camera down from the ceiling—all tubes and levers and ribbed black tubing. At last he seemed satisfied and went back to the control panels. I seized my opportunity and hurried round to Alec's right-hand side. Crouching behind the trolley where the X-ray technician couldn't see me, I refitted the syringe to the bung at Alec's wrist and began pressing on the plunger with both hands. My thumbs blanched with the effort. My fingers were white claws around the flanges of the syringe. So intent was I on getting the lethal fluid into Alec's veins that I didn't notice the door behind me opening. I looked up and found Thorn standing behind me.

"What exactly are you doing?"

I released the syringe. I'd hardly had time to inject anything.

"The drip's blocked," I said. "I'm just flushing it through with saline."

He took the syringe out of my hands. "Fifty mills seems a bit excessive." Then he switched on the drip. It was running perfectly.

Jenny came in through the swing doors and Thorn gave her the syringe to dispose of. He was already taking off his jacket and stooping over Alec's body. His thin, quick fingers explored the head and neck, ran over both arms and under Alec's back. He pinched a toe, tapped a couple of reflexes, threw away my Guedel's airway and put a finger in Alec's mouth.

"E-T tube," he said.

Jenny snapped to it and brought him back a cuffed tube and a laryngoscope. Thorn pulled back Alec's head, extended the neck, pulled up the handle of the laryngoscope and slipped in the tube.

Jenny hooked up the oxygen and started pumping the Ambou bag.

"Blood pressure?" Thorn was speaking to me.

"I don't know."

"Take it," he said. "Then replace that saline with Haemmaccel."

I did what I was told. The technician waited in the wings for his cue. Everything was slipping out of my control—the student nurse had finished shaving Alec's leg and had now taken over the Ambou bag. Thorn was listening to Alec's chest and tapping with one finger over his spleen. Jenny was slipping the Thomas splint over Alec's left leg. I put up the Haemmaccel as the surgical SHO arrived, cursing my lost chance—for a few minutes Alec's life had been hanging by a thread. Now, suddenly, his survival looked assured. I drew off some blood samples, watching gloomily as the orthopedic SHO wrapped Alec's left leg in a damp dressing. The rest of the team moved around him, prodding and testing, flashing lights and tapping reflexes, pumping the blood-pressure cuffs and moving their stethoscopes like chess pieces over his chest and abdomen.

I left resus and went to see the minor cases who'd been waiting all this time. I can't even remember what was wrong with them. All my concentration was focused on the resuscitation room. I had the insane idea that any minute Alec would suddenly regain consciousness and sit up in the trolley saying I'd tried to kill him.

Of course he didn't. Thorn put in a chest drain and the orthopaedic SHO inserted traction pins. Gradually the activity around Alec's bed subsided. The surgical

SHO went back to bed and the X-ray technician developed his last film. I caught a final glimpse of my victim as his trolley was wheeled out, creaking and clanking up the corridor toward the service lifts with a person on either side holding a drip bag in the air and the blood from Alec's chest collecting in a small glass jar.

CHAPTER 35

14th July

Dear Simon,
It struck me after all this time that I'd left quite a lot of
bills unpaid—telephone, gas, etc. I guess we all forget
details in a crisis. Check enclosed for £150. Hope this
covers it.

I'm sorry about the way I left. I know it was pretty
abrupt but if 'twere done 'tis best 'twere done quickly. I
hate deception and I know you do. Hope all's well and
the Mountford cloud has blown over and your world's
going OK.

I'm living in Notting Hill Gate and about to start
work on a play at the Bush which a friend of mine is
directing—an adaptation of The Good Soldier.

Ashburnham is being played by a bloke called Paul Davies. Do you know him? Apparently he went to Cambridge the same time as you. I'm meeting him tomorrow at the read-through.

Come and see the play if you're ever in London. It's on from the 1st till the 14th of September.

Yours,
Christine

CHAPTER
36

LYING IN THE FLAT I COULD hear the dawn approaching—the irritating chattering of sparrows under the eaves, a bothersome reminder that time was rolling on. I'd been awake all night and felt light-headed from lack of sleep. Soon the milk car would be arriving. Soon the lights would go on in the hospital across the Gorge. Soon the morning ward round would reach Alec and the course of his recovery would be planned.

I was dressed by seven and spent the next two hours pacing up and down in the lounge trying to engage the stripped gears of rational thought. At nine I heard the post arriving and went downstairs to collect it. The letter was the last thing I needed—across the Gorge a man I'd tried to kill was being nursed back to health and now, somewhere in London, Christine was meeting with a man who might know Hennessey.

I had to think. I'd coped with crises in the past and I could cope with this one. There was nothing I could do about Christine. There was something I could do about Alec.

I phoned the intensive-care unit. They told me he was stable on the respirator. Until his crushed chest improved there was no chance of his talking, conscious or not. Maybe I had nothing to worry about—I knew that head injuries often lost all recollection of the circumstances immediately preceding their accident. A bash such as Alec's might erase all that had happened in the three or four hours before I ran him over.

Still, I couldn't bank on it. And if I was going to finish him off, then now, while he was lying defenseless in intensive care, seemed the best time to do it.

The question was how. The Marcaine was too bulky and he'd survived a small bolus of the stuff. I needed something neater. It needed to be quick. It needed to be untraceable. And I needed to do it soon.

I looked up "Poisons" in Davidson's *Principles and Practice of Medicine* but it wasn't much use to me. It was all about tablets that people might overdose on and I knew most of it already from my experience in the Accident Department: Paracetamol worked too slowly, aspirin overdose was too easily detectable. Mogadon was almost completely harmless and giving tablets to an unconscious man was pretty impossible anyway.

I needed something I could inject, which gave me the choice between barbiturates and opiates. Heroin came in the smallest lethal dose and would probably therefore be easiest to smuggle into the department, but hospital supplies of heroin are carefully monitored. If I took any from the Accident Department it would be logged. On top of that there was the chance that, at postmortem, they'd detect its presence in his blood—there had to be something else.

I dragged myself into work in the afternoon and spent every spare minute trying to focus on the textbooks. I returned to the flat no farther forward. Time was running out—every moment I delayed, the chances of his regaining consciousness increased. I paced around Christine's flat, smoking, chewing my nails, watching the traffic on the overpass below streaming westward. In an effort to settle my nerves I drank three or four glasses of gin but only succeeded in further distorting my perception.

I went to the bathroom and splashed water on my face. I reached blindly for the towel and then it struck me.

"Potassium."

I splashed more water on and dried my face, massaging the soreness out of my eyes.

"Potassium, of course."

Fear is a drug. Under its influence the mind makes strange leaps, impossible connections. I remembered delivering a lab result at the West Harwood. The doctor who received it, a short Jewish man with a bald patch, scanning through them and saying, "Ah, potassium six point five, that would kill you and me."

Potassium! It was perfect: a natural component of plasma, colorless, painless, injectable and lethal in relatively small doses. I wondered why I hadn't thought of it before.

It was dark outside. I snatched my stethoscope off the table, stuffed it in my jacket pocket and made my way back across the bridge.

In the soft blue light of the intensive-care unit the nurses moved liked ghosts: measuring, charting and adjusting— a precise ballet of concern to the glottal click and hiss of the respirators. The nurses' activity provided the percussion—the crackle of a starched dress, the scratch of a pen on a chart, the squeak of rubber on linoleum.

"You are?" The male nurse was a slightly built man with fair, curly hair and red-rimmed eyes.

"Dr. Hennessey," I said.

"And you've come to see?"

"Alec Moran."

"Who?"

"The road accident . . ." I said quickly, "I admitted him last night."

"He's not called Alec."

"Someone said . . . I think I heard . . ." I stammered and tailed off, grateful for the high paper mask that concealed my face. "How is he?"

"He's called Matthew. Matthew Harris."

"Called what?"

The sleeplessness, the heat, and the bizarre setting all heightened the dreamlike quality of this conversation. I looked across to where Alec lay, half expecting to see myself on the bed.

"How did they identify him?" I asked.

"He had a cigarette case in his pocket. The police are looking for relatives."

My cigarette case! I remembered leaving the West Harwood, disposing of everything that bore my name. I'd given it to him then.

"By the window," said the nurse, "Call me if you need any help."

I needed help all right. I wondered if they'd manage to trace my mother. Or if she'd be called on to identify the body.

I approached Alec warily. The warm air was beginning to make my skin itch under the sterile paper gown. As an orderly I'd always felt too big, too dirty, too physical for intensive care.

There were six beds and four of them were occupied. There were no screens—few patients who came here were in a condition to feel embarrassed about their nudity. Alec's face and head had been shaved so that, even close up, I hardly recognized him. In unconsciousness he looked like a learned, almost spiritual person. If I had ever seen him like that before I might have taken his opinions more seriously.

His left leg was encased in plaster to the thigh; his right was suspended in traction by way of a pin through the shin just below the knee. A catheter emerged from between the folds of his small, reclusive penis and drained into a bag by his bedside. Another tube ran from his chest on the left into a glass bottle, now a quarter filled with blood. The skin of his chest and abdomen had taken on a tense, lacquered gloss, straining on the long scar through which they'd removed his spleen. A ribbed tracheostomy tube ran from his throat to the wheezing chrome device at his bedside.

I took the visitor's chair and placed it near the head of his bed. I couldn't get near for the various drips and had to lean foward to see him properly. Beyond the venetian blinds the outline of the suspension bridge was drawn in colored lights.

A nurse came and started fussing about with the leads to Alec's cardiac monitor so I picked up the in-patient notes at the end of his bed and read, in various handwritings, the story of his admission and the various operations that had been performed on him through the previous night—so much wasted effort: Thorn with his admission and the draining of the chest; Sparkes the orthopedic resident on the cleaning and plastering of the right leg; David Nixon from surgery on the removal of his ruptured spleen; Thorn again with an interim neuro assessment; then Alan Stevenson, the radiographer, with the results of an emergency CAT scan. The last small entries were the progress notes written by the anesthetics SHO. I wondered as I thumbed the pages how the story of Alec's life would look: his mother on his boisterious childhood; some teacher in Greenock on his unremarkable school career; his Clydeside foreman on his apprenticeship as a fitter; Slattery's contribution on behalf of the NHS and, finally, my own smudged comments on his premature death.

I'd been doing a bit of reading on the subject of potassium. Apparently it had a cumulative effect so I didn't have to risk injecting Alec with it while he lay there. I merely had to spike the bag of intravenous fluid which was laid out ready to go up. Sometime during the four hours it took to run through, Alec would have a heart attack. I'd be safely out of the way.

The cardiac monitor had settled. The nurse reset the alarm limits and left. Unnoticed in the twilight I took the bag of saline off Alec's bedside table and smuggled it under the folds of my paper gown. With one hand I found the rubber injection portal, with the other I got the syringe of potassium out of my pocket. I pierced the bung and injected the potassium through it. The bag felt slightly more tense than it should have but not tense enough to draw attention. I replaced the bag on the table, pocketed the empty syringe and looked behind me. The nurses were going about their business, too busy with replacing someone's sheets to bother about me.

I sat by Alec a while longer. The current bag of saline was virtually run through and I wanted to see this one go up. I watched his chest inflating and deflating in time with the pump. I put out a hand and touched his waxy skin. There was, of course, no response. Even if he was conscious the paralytic that prevented him from coughing against the respirator would make it impossible for him to move. His eyes were taped shut with thin strips of transparent tape to protect the corneas.

Eventually the nurse came back. I saw her take down the empty drip bag and replace it with one I'd already doctored. I lingered behind to see the first drips run through—the initial seconds of Alec's four-hour death sentence. While I waited, the male charge nurse came back and busied himself around Alec's bed, recording his pulse, blood pressure, temperature and urine output, then writing them down on the daily chart. It did add a mathematical neatness to the process of dying. So different from the noisy battles that took place on the ground floor. I was glad that Alec should die here rather than down there. I was still haunted by visions of Celia Mountford's inelegant demise. In contrast, there was something almost religious about Alec's waxy, bloated form, spread-eagled in the half light, drifting off into oblivion to the music of the cardiac monitor.

I walked back across the bridge, contemplating my remaining problems. Alec had been for an interview at the Royal Clifton. Would someone realize his true identity? And how far would the police pursue the Matthew Harris lead? With Matthew Harris dead was I worse or better off? I was so preoccupied as I walked up the crescent that I didn't notice the lights were on in the flat.

CHAPTER 37

WHEN I WAS SIX STEPS FROM the door I realized someone was waiting for me. There was a chink of light just visible under the draft excluder and as I drew closer I could hear someone playing Ry Cooder. It was one of the records that Christine had left behind.

I found her sitting in her favorite position on the pink sofa, drinking whiskey. She was wearing jeans and a bandsman's jacket with heavy gold epaulets and braid down the front. She had cut her hair short. It suited her.

"Hello, stranger," she said.

I tried to smile but had lost control of the muscles of my face. I managed a twisted grin.

"You look a bit wild," she said. "What have you been doing?"

"Looking after someone," I said.

"Successful?"

"I think so."

She sipped her coffee, watching me the way her cat used to.

"How's London?" I asked.

"Good."

"How was the read-through for your play?"

"The play's fine."

"I've forgotten what it was called," I said.

"It's an adaptation of *The Good Soldier.*"

"I've never heard of it."

"It's a book by Ford Madox Ford. You'd like it. It's about dishonesty." It was difficult to read her expression in the firelight but there was no obvious barb. "I'm playing Florence," she continued. "I die in the second half."

"Too bad."

She shrugged. "Up till then it's a very good part."

"So what brings you down here?" I asked.

"You obviously got my letter."

"Yes."

"Well?"

"Thanks for the money," I said.

She smiled indulgently. "I meant, do you know Paul Davies?"

"No."

"He knows you," she said.

"Oh, yes."

"He went to your funeral."

A spark flew onto the rug and I stamped on it, aware that she was watching me very intently now. I attempted an expression of amused incomprehension but couldn't quite achieve it. "He must be confusing me with someone else."

"I don't think so," said Christine.

"Well, I'm alive, aren't I?"

"So you are," she said.

I measured the distance between myself and Christine, then between Christine and the door. I was amazed how unafraid she looked until I remembered that she didn't know about Alec. I picked up the poker and stirred the logs in the fire.

"You don't believe in miracles," I told her.

"No," she said, "not anymore."

"So there's obviously some mistake."

"Yes, yes, that's what I said. But the fact is he'd described you almost exactly—he knew you went to Filbourne, that your parents lived in Surrey, that you went to Clare College. . . . I mean, how many Dr. Simon Hennesseys are there?"

"Obviously more than one."

"You reckon?"

"Well, there's got to be an explanation, hasn't there?"

"There is an explanation."

"Namely?"

"That you're not who you say you are."

I laughed unconvincingly. "Old Paul Davies," I said. "He was pulling your leg."

"No, he wasn't. I checked with the West Harwood and with Clare College, Cambridge. How much more proof do I need? I even went down Portobello Road. There's a shop called Handle With Care. You remember the first time we made love, you were talking about that? There's a woman called Mrs. Harris who runs it. Her son's called Matthew. He's got dark hair and green eyes. He's a theater orderly. She showed me his picture."

I felt I was floating in space—the game was up. "You told her then."

"No."

"You told this Paul Davies guy?"

"I didn't tell anyone. I just asked if he knew you and he volunteered the rest," she said. "I didn't say anything—I wanted to talk to you first."

The fire growled. I poked it some more. "That's very brave of you."

"What should I be scared of?"

"You're the only person who knows."

"What are you going to do?" She laughed. "Kill me?"

"I killed Celia Mountford," I said.

"That was different."

"In law it would be murder."

She shook her head. "Manslaughter," she said. "You're not capable of murder."

"People change."

"I still don't believe that," she said.

"So, are you planning to call the police?" I asked.

"I've no idea, I haven't thought it through yet. I wanted to get to know you."

"You already know me. We were very close in a way."

"Not really. We didn't have a very truthful relationship, did we?"

"It seemed truthful."

She smiled and took off her jacket. She was wearing a tailored blouse which showed off her figure. "'If for nine years I have possessed a goodly apple that is rotten to the core and discover its rottenness only after nine years and six days, isn't it true to say that for nine years I possessed a goodly apple?'"

"What's that?"

"It's from the play." She stretched her bare arms along the back of the couch. "Didn't you suspect anything?"

"Me?" I said. "Suspect what?"

"All that stuff about my Uncle Jack. How I had to go and visit him every other weekend and he wasn't on the phone?"

I shrugged. "It seemed perfectly plausible."

She fiddled with the braid on the cuff of her jacket where part of the stitching had come loose. "You remember I had a photograph, the first time you came here? It was over there in a Perspex frame."

"The man with the beard?" I said.

"He's called Justin. He's a theater director. We've had one of these on-off affairs for years. It was during a low point in that that I decided the nuns were right and I should have been a nurse. But I lacked your confidence. I never really cast adrift. I used to carry on seeing him every weekend. He was my secret escape route. I could sit on the fence. And it worked just fine till you came along and I began to feel attracted to you. Justin guessed what was going on and decided to finish it between us."

I remembered the letter and her tearful return from London.

"So it was all bullshit, that stuff about your dying uncle?"

"Well, it was based on truth. The best lies are based on truth, I don't have to tell you that. My Uncle Jack did have cancer of the prostate. And I did used to visit him a lot. But he'd been dead for four years when I met you."

"And in the end you chose Justin in preference to me."

She smiled. "Actually I was quite happy with both of you. But in the end I chose acting. The Mountford business was what decided it. If that hadn't happened I'd probably still be leading a double life."

"Sorry I messed things up for you," I said.

"Not at all. It was bound to happen. That's the only guarantee of morality, isn't it—the traps we set for ourselves?"

I laughed without humor. "You think I want to be caught?"

"I don't know," she said. "It must be incredibly stressful keeping up the pretense."

"It is," I said.

"What would you have done if I hadn't turned up?"

"Actually I was planning to kill myself."

She looked into my eyes, probing my expression for sincerity. "You're lying."

I met her gaze, high on fear and exhaustion. The

joint between fact and fiction had finally become seamless. This was someone else talking. "I don't mean kill me," I said. "I mean kill Matthew Harris."

"What good is that going to do?"

"I guess it'll keep me honest," I said. "You talk about setting traps for yourself. My problem is I haven't laid any. I'm like you were. I'm sitting on the fence. If anything goes terribly wrong I can just revert to my old identity. If I get rid of Matthew Harris I can't afford mistakes, can I?"

"How were you thinking of killing him off?"

"There's an unidentified guy on the critical list in the ICU. I slipped my old cigarette case into his pocket the night he came in. He's Matthew Harris now."

After a pause she said, "They'll need someone to identify him."

I left the fire and sat down beside her. "How about it then?"

"Who, me?"

"You're an actress. You could pretend to be my sister and report me missing."

She laughed out loud. "Why do you think I'd want to get involved in something like this?"

I stroked the edge of her ear and, behind it, the fine cropped ends of her hair. "Just for old times' sake."

"You must be crazy," she said.

"I suppose I must be. Have some more whiskey."

"I'd never get away with it."

"Sure you would."

She drained her own glass and held it out for more. "Tell me about your sister," she said.

CHAPTER
38

WE MADE LOVE TILL THREE IN the morning and Christine left on the early train. Now, lying in the middle of the bed, squinting at the sunlight on the ceiling, the events of the previous evening seemed profoundly unlikely. I got up and walked through the lounge. The ashes on the fire were scattered around the grate. The bottle of Glenfiddich stood on the carpet, almost empty. The dish of ice cubes had melted. There was a scribbled note from Christine (*Will be in touch, see you, C.*). I cleaned up the fire and threw on the remains of the ice cubes to keep the ashes down. Then I dialed the hospital and asked for the ICU.

"Intensive care—staff nurse speaking."
"Hello, I'm phoning about the RTA who came in last night."

"Are you a relative?"

"No, it's Dr. Hennessey, the casualty officer. I admitted him."

"Now, Dr. Hennessey, you know we're not allowed to give information over the phone. I could be speaking to anyone, couldn't I?"

"I know. I said I'm sorry, I was just worried about him."

"Well," she said. ". . . in fact he went into asystole at four-twenty this morning. We couldn't bring him round."

"Do you have any idea why he died?"

"Yes. They reckon it was potassium poisoning."

"Do they?" I tried to sound casually interested. "Why do they think that?"

"It's a common side effect of massive blood transfusion."

"Of course." I almost laughed with relief. "Of course it is." I rattled the receiver back onto the phone.

Fueled by adrenaline I ran all the way down the stairs, round the crescent, up the hill to the corner shop and back again. I cooked myself bacon and eggs while I worked out a plan of action.

At nine-thirty I rang the hospital again and asked to speak to the nursing chief, who was called Mrs. Russell. Her Bristol accent was even thicker than Molly's, effectively obliterating all her vowel sounds so that when she introduced herself on the phone it sounded like "Mrs. Arsehole" and I had to ask her to repeat it.

In turn I tried to imitate Alec's Glasgow accent. "Hello," I said. "This is Alec Moran speaking. I'm due to be starting with you in a couple of days."

"Oh, yes."

"Look. I don't know how to tell you this but I've decided against it."

"You're not coming then?"

"No."

"You've been offered another job, have you?"

"No, I've just decided I'm not cut out for nursing."

I imagined I could hear the sound of her breathing. She eventually said, "So what will you do instead?"

I hadn't been prepared for this so I blurted out, "I fancied working in the theater—I've been offered a part in a play."

"Oh, yes."

"So I'm afraid I'll have to pull out."

There was a long silence. "Well," said Mrs. Russell, "I don't exactly know what to say. I imagine you realize you're putting us in an impossible position but if that's the way you feel . . ."

There were a couple more exchanges in which I became progressively more humble. Eventually she put the phone down very abruptly.

I put on a tie and went in to work. There was nothing to do now but wait.

CHAPTER
39

24th July

Dear Simon,
I suppose I should call you Matthew but I feel I know Simon better.

Well, mission accomplished. I phoned up the police in Notting Hill and told them my brother, Matthew, hadn't turned up for a few days. They sent a detective round to interview me which was pretty grueling—I hope you appreciate all this. I had to rent a hotel room, pack a suitcase, all that stuff. I have this blond wig for the play so I wore that with some false suntan. I looked like a real tart.

I told them I'd had an appointment to meet you in London, that you'd phoned me a couple of weeks pre-

224

viously to confirm it and you were normally pretty reliable. I said you had no permanent address and I had no idea where you'd been for the last three months. The policeman obviously thought I was wasting his time but he said he'd make some inquiries. I got a call the next evening to say you'd been located in Bristol.

The identification was a bit hairy. I had to come down to the Royal Clifton for the morning. I was only in the hospital for half an hour but I was terrified that someone would see through my disguise. They showed me the Matthew Harris body and I said, yes, that was you. I thought the policeman would never let me get away. He wanted to know all sorts of things—what kind of bloke you were, whether I knew of any close friends of yours. I said, no, you were a loner and a drifter, that you'd never formed any close attachments and never stuck in a job for long. I shed a few tears and they packed me off in a taxi with a form to apply for traveling expenses. I headed straight for the station and got the train back to London. I didn't even phone you, I was feeling so paranoid. It's terrifying. I don't know how you manage to live like this.

Anyway I burned the clothes and the wig so if anything goes wrong I don't know anything about you. I feel I've done my bit. Hope you appreciate it.

Good luck with the new job. If they ever catch up with you, then don't, for God's sake, mention my name. I've taken the rap for you once already and that's quite enough. I imagine you'll eventually become a consultant and make a fortune—you have all the right qualities.

So long,
Christine, XX

CHAPTER
40

ORDER OUT OF CHAOS.

Many times during my final week at the Royal Clifton Hospital I reflected on how conveniently everything had worked out. Matthew Harris was officially dead and Alec Moran had disappeared. I had finally carved myself free from my past. I knew I could rely on Christine to keep my secret. Her brief involvement in the process of deception would ensure that. I was on day shift for the last week of July. At night I slept easy.

On the thirty-first I packed my few belongings in the back of the car and prepared for the short journey south. I had the oil and water checked at the garage at the top of The Mall and drove back into the hospital to say goodbye to my friends.

I'd never got it together with Andrea. She'd given up on me when I ditched her in the swimming pool and taken up with one of the gynecology residents. Still, she seemed sorry enough to see me go and we promised to keep in touch. I said good-bye to Kassim who was heading off to do VSO and to Adam who had a GP rotation fixed up in Taunton. Hillary and Gareth were staying on in Bristol for another six months. They said they might visit me in Salisbury.

Before I left I paid a final visit to my old room in the doctors' home. I'd not stayed there for several weeks but Molly had stubbornly continued to treat the place as though I was still in residence. There were flowers in the window and a clean towel by the sink. It's quite possible that all the time I stayed at Christine's she'd continued to leave cups of sweet tea by the bedside. I sat on the bed with my jacket on. Why had I come back here? Nostalgia? Surely not. A faint red mud stain was still visible on the carpet. I felt the bedsprings and thought about Christine.

"You going then, or what?"

Molly was standing in the doorway. She had a dustpan and brush in one hand and a red bandanna on her head.

I stood up. "Yes, I'm going."

"What you come back here for?"

"I'm not quite sure," I said.

She came into the room and began hauling the covers off the bed. "I'm giving this place a cleanout for the next doctor. I thought I'd seen the last of you."

"You have." I got up to leave.

"What's your forwarding address?"

"No forwarding address."

"What if some mail comes?"

"Chuck it away," I told her. "Bye-bye now."

I patted her on the head as I left. The gesture was designed to annoy her and seemed to achieve that effect.

I looked up as I left the residence and saw her scowling through the window at me—a small malevolent face, framed by wisteria. Then she turned away to begin her cleaning program.

Having won the final point against Molly I decided to try my luck with Thorn. I felt it would be a sporting gesture, like shaking hands with one's adversary after a protracted and vicious contest. As the victor it was the least I could do.

I knocked and entered. The window of his office was open. Outside, the warm air was dense with pollen. Inside, Thorn was hunched over a wad of lab reports, scowling over his glasses.

I swung the door shut and strode over to his desk. I was wearing a loose sleeveless shirt outside my jeans—casual to the point of insolence.

He looked up and said, "Well?"

"Hello," I said breezily. "Just came to say good-bye."

"Good-bye, Hennessey." He immediately returned to his notes. I chuckled lightly. He wasn't getting off that easily.

"I wanted to tell you how much I've enjoyed working in the department and to wish you all the best in the future."

"Did you indeed?" He was still studying the notes. I realized he wasn't going to shake my hand and I felt a sudden urge to grab his big noble head and bash it on the desk.

Instead I said, "You don't like me, do you?"

That got his attention. He put down his pen and looked at me long and hard, as though considering this.

"I've done my job," I said. "I've been doing it for six months. I was a bit shaky at first and I had some bad luck with Mrs. Mountford but otherwise you've had no cause for complaint."

He took off his glasses and pinched the bridge of his nose. "What's your problem, Hennessey?"

"You never seem satisfied," I said. I'd embarked on this hoping to be laconic but the more I thought about it the more angry I became. "You're incredibly rude to me. You only ever seem to pick up on my mistakes. Why is that? I'm not the worst doctor in the world by a long way."

He smiled at me without humor. "You're right, I've had worse casualty officers than you. Two that I can think of—I sacked both of them."

"Well, why didn't you sack me then?"

"Maybe I should have . . . in fact I should never have hired you. I was sort of pressured into it by poor old Mountford—he was always rather elitist about Oxbridge graduates. I kept telling him to look beyond the qualifications, to look at the person . . . still . . ."

He turned to look out of the window, at the clouds of pollen blowing off the pines. I could feel myself breathing quickly. "So what didn't you like about me?"

He turned back and considered me through those implacable, baggy eyes. "I'll tell you what I think it is," he said. "You don't care."

He waited to see if this registered. It didn't.

"Like you say, you can do the job well enough but I get the impression you don't care about people. I've felt that ever since you first came to the interview. In fact I said it to you then, if you remember, that we don't want high-flyers, that I couldn't give a damn about paper qualifications. I wanted someone who cared—who cared about the job, cared about the hospital, cared about the people. And I get the impression, Hennessey, that you don't. Oh, you care about the impression you make. You care about whether I like you. But you don't genuinely care about anyone who comes through this department. You didn't care about Celia Mountford. Or Benny, or that nurse who resigned on your behalf . . . You see, it's not the white coat and the stethoscope and the bleeper that make a doctor. It's that ability to be concerned about others. Which you don't have."

I was silent. He leaned back.

"That's why I dislike you . . . that central emptiness. You work only for yourself. You don't give that"—he clicked his fingers at me—"for the little people."

I grinned and shook my head. He was talking nonsense. What was I doing here? I didn't need his approval. He could think what he liked—I was never going to see him again. "At least you're honest," I said.

He checked his watch. "Now, if you'll excuse me, I have a ward round to attend to." He started gathering up the notes and filing them away.

I turned toward the door. "Good-bye then."

"Good-bye, Dr. Hennessey."

The bastard.

Driving down the A36 I had time to reflect on what he had said. "Central emptiness" he had called it. Well, maybe there was something wrong with me. Christine had always said I had a screw missing. Alec had once called it constitutional selfishness. Molly hadn't bothered to articulate it but she was obviously responding to the same thing. Maybe I'd been born with it. You can be born physically handicapped. Maybe an emotional handicap was feasible.

So what? "The little people"? Who the hell were they anyway? Who gives a toss about them? I say, piss on the little people. Think big and go for it. Morality is just a form of cowardice. Give me a passport and a credit card and the world's my oyster.

I slammed on the brakes and threw the car onto the soft shoulder.

My passport. My bloody passport.

I waited for two cars to pass, then reversed into a lay-by. It was three-forty-five. I performed a tight U-turn, mounted the opposite verge, then put my foot down and headed back in the direction I'd come from.

In fifteen minutes I'd be back in Bristol.

CHAPTER
41

31st July
3 p.m.

Attention Dr. Thorn:
This brown envelope was found while cleaning room of
Dr. Hennessey. (Taped behind wardrobe.) No forward-
ing address, so have opened it. Contains passport, etc.
(?Important.)

Signed,
Molly S. Williams (Housekeeper)